## THE GOOD MASTER
Written and illustrated by Kate Seredy

On the Good Master's ranch there were thousands of sheep, cattle, and horses, but no friend for his son, Jancsi. Jancsi would have given ten horses for a boy, he would even give a donkey for a girl. So when he heard that his cousin Kate was coming from Budapest to stay with his family, he was thrilled. Then Kate arrived, a spoiled and headstrong city girl—and she fought with Jancsi from the moment they met. But the kindly understanding of the Good Master would calm her temper, and meanwhile Kate and Jancsi could enjoy all that life on the ranch had to offer: horseback races across the plains, country fairs, and new friends, like the shepherd who made wood carvings and whose tales kept the children listening till sundown.

The story of Kate's stay on the ranch covers a glorious round of seasons—lambing time and harvest, the round-up of the horses, country festivals—and each has its own thrills and its novelty for the city girl. The feeling of color and scene is delightfully presented and carries the reader right inside a world few of us have ever known. The pictures beautifully fill out the scenes that the author describes so vividly.

# THE
# GOOD MASTER

*WRITTEN AND ILLUSTRATED BY*

KATE SEREDY

PUFFIN BOOKS

*To the wise, kind, and tolerant good master*

DR. WILLIAM MANNINGER

*this book is dedicated, to say:* Thank you

PUFFIN BOOKS
Published by the Penguin Group
Penguin Putnam Inc., 375 Hudson Street, New York, New York 10014, U.S.A.
Penguin Books Ltd, 27 Wrights Lane, London W8 5TZ, England
Penguin Books Australia Ltd, Ringwood, Victoria, Australia
Penguin Books Canada Ltd, 10 Alcorn Avenue, Toronto, Ontario, Canada M4V 3B2
Penguin Books (N.Z.) Ltd, 182–190 Wairau Road, Auckland 10, New Zealand

Penguin Books Ltd, Registered Offices: Harmondsworth, Middlesex, England

First published by Viking Penguin Inc. 1935
Published in Puffin Books 1986
50  49  48  47  46  45
Copyright Kate Seredy 1935
Copyright © renewed Kate Seredy, 1963
All rights reserved

Printed in U.S.A.

Library of Congress Cataloging in Publication Data
Seredy, Kate.      The good master.
Originally published: New York: Viking Press, 1935.
Summary: Two cousins spend an adventurous summer on a ranch on the Hungarian plains.
[1. Cousins—Fiction.   2. Hungary—Fiction]   I. Title.
PZ7.S48Go  1986     [Fic]     85-43043     ISBN 0-14-030133-X

# CONTENTS

# LIST OF FULL PAGE DRAWINGS

# CHAPTER I

## *COUSIN KATE FROM BUDAPEST*

JANCSI was up bright and early that morning and at work milking the cows. He was so excited he couldn't stay in bed. For today Cousin Kate was coming. She was the only cousin he had, and she was a city girl. A real city girl from Budapest. Ever since the letter came from his uncle, Jancsi had been the proudest boy on the big Hungarian plain. He was the only boy in the neighborhood who had a cousin in the city. And she was coming today, to stay for a long time. Father had told Jancsi what was in the letter. It said that Kate had had the measles last winter. Jancsi had never had the measles—he thought it must be something wonderful to have. And she was delicate, the letter said, too, so she was coming to the country. A *delicate* city cousin, who had had the *measles*—that was something.

If it were only Sunday, they would go to church and he could tell everybody about her. Sunday was the only time when Jancsi saw anyone outside his own family. Father had a ranch, with thousands of sheep, horses, cows, and pigs. He had chickens and ducks and geese; he even had donkeys, but he didn't have enough children to suit Jancsi. It got *so* lonesome for poor Jancsi, he would have given ten horses for a brother. He had it all figured out—he would give a donkey for even a sister. Not horses, just a donkey.

The ranch was miles and miles from the village. It was too far to walk, and they were too busy to drive on weekdays. So, although Jancsi was ten years old and quite a man if you asked his opinion, he had never been to school, and he did not know how to read or write. The ranch was the only reality to him—the world outside was just a fairy story. Mother knew lots of fairy stories about dragons and golden-haired princesses who lived in glittering castles. Jancsi thought that houses in Budapest were made of gold and had diamond windows. All the city people rode around on pure white horses and wore silk gowns. Cousin Kate would have golden curls, rosy cheeks, big blue eyes; she would wear a white silk flowing gown, and her voice would be like honey. Now—Jancsi is off in dreamland— some day a dragon will capture her, and it will be up to Jancsi to go to the rescue. He is clad in green velvet, red boots, riding a coal-black steed. Here comes the dragon! Jancsi pulls out his golden sword, and one-two-three heads are at his feet! All good dragons have twelve perfectly hideous heads. Four—slash, five—swish goes his sword ——

"Mo-o-o-o!" bellowed something close to him. And crash-bang went Jancsi together with the milking-stool. He sat and blinked. Máli, the mottled cow, looked at him with reproachful eyes. Reality closed around the hero—oh yes, here he was in the barn, milking the cow.

"Jancsi! Ja-a-ncsi-i! Hurry up with the milk or you'll be late for the train!" It was his mother's voice calling from the house. He scrambled to his feet, scowled at Máli, and picking up the full pails made his way back to the kitchen. Mother took the milk from him. "I'll strain it today, Jancsi. You eat your breakfast and get dressed. And get a good scrub—why, you're all full of mud!"

Jancsi kept his back out of Mother's sight—the seat of his white pants would need explaining. He gulped down his bread and milk. Then, backing out of the kitchen, he ran to the well. He filled a wooden bucket with the icy water and, stripping off his clothes, stepped into it. With great splutters and groans he scrubbed himself, using sand on the most disgraceful spots. Then he took a bit of salt from a mug and scrubbed his teeth with his fingers. Squirting out the salty water, he set a new long-distance record; he even paused long enough to gaze at it admiringly and mark the spot with a stone. "Can spit almost as far as Father," he muttered with pride.

He ran back to the house. His very best Sunday clothes were all laid out on the bench, near the big white stove—his embroidered shirt, the wide pleated pants, his shiny black boots, his round hat with the bunch of flowers. He put them on. Mother wasn't in the kitchen. He went to the bedroom. No Mother in the bedroom. But on the windowsill, glittering in the sunshine, was a green bottle. He gazed at it for a while, torn between desire and discipline. It was too much for him. Tiptoeing to the window, he took the bottle and the little red comb next to it. It was perfumed hair oil—and only *men* used perfumed hair oil! He put a little on his hair. Then a little more, and still more, until his hair looked as if it were made of black enamel. Then with a sigh of satisfaction he put on his hat and strutted out. He heard the wagon—time to go!

When he saw the wagon drive up to the door, he gave a whoop of joy. Father had harnessed his four black horses with the very best brass-studded harness. Each horse had a big bunch of geraniums fastened to the headband, and long streamers of gayly colored ribbons floated in the breeze. He jumped up next to Father, and off they went down the long poplar-lined lane leading to the main road.

It was early April, and fields and pastures were a fresh pale green. The poplars stood like solemn sentinels, whispering to the wind. Father was a man of few words; men never spoke, he believed, unless they had something important to say. Gossip was only for the womenfolks. Jancsi was quiet, too, busy with his own thoughts. He was going to the town for the first time in his life—he would see a train. Trains were a mystery to him.

One of the shepherds had told him trains were fire-eating dragons; they roared, and snorted black smoke. "They pull little houses; people go from one place to another in the little houses. And trains kill everybody who gets in their way." Jancsi wondered if he could hitch their own house to one of these dragons. Then he could go and see the world. But he would take his dog Peti, he'd take his favorite horse, he'd take Máli, the cow . . . No, he scowled and rubbed his side, remembering this morning. No, he wouldn't take Máli. Deeply absorbed in deciding whom he would take with him, he hardly noticed how fast they were traveling. Soon they left the open country and entered the long village street. The village was always interesting to him, so he began to look around. Father turned to him. "I'll stop at the store to buy some tobacco. You hold the reins, Jancsi." Jancsi slid over to Father's seat and grabbed the reins. He sat there, head up, shoulders erect, looking straight ahead. Just then a village boy walked by. He stopped and looked at Jancsi with open admiration.

"Hey! You driving *alone?*"

Jancsi gulped and replied evasively: "Going to fetch my cousin from the train. She comes from Budapest." Then, unable to keep from gossiping like womenfolks, he blurted out his news: "She had the measles and is delicate and her name is Kate! She'll live with us!"

Father came down the store steps, stuffing his pipe. Jancsi prayed for a miracle. If the boy would only go away or if Father would only let him drive . . . !

The miracle came. Father walked around the wagon and, getting up next to Jancsi, said: "Let's see how you handle wagon and four!"

So they left the boy staring after them open-mouthed. Jancsi drove through the village like a king in a golden coach. The clouds of white dust around the horses' hoofs were like stardust to him. The glittering hoofs were made of diamonds. Everything looked new and beautiful to him today. The endless rows of snow-white houses with their gayly painted doors and shutters were like pearls in a row. The geraniums in the windows were a brighter red than ever. The church seemed taller, the grass greener. He flipped his whip impatiently at the barking dogs and almost rode over a flock of honking geese slowly plodding across the street. Then they were in the open country again. It was almost noon; the spring sun beat down on the shimmering fields. They passed a long fence. Horses were grazing placidly in the pasture.

"Good horseflesh," remarked Father. "See how meek they look now, but it's a man's job to stay on one of those beasts."

"I can get on one and stay on it, Father. Those aren't worse than your own horses."

"Think you can, Son?"

"I *know* I can!" asserted Jancsi hastily, forgetting that this would call for explanations. He was not yet allowed to ride unbroken horses.

"You *know* you can?" said Father, reaching for his pocket knife. Jancsi watched him in shocked silence. He knew he was in for it, but somehow he didn't mind. After the pocket knife came a little round stick of wood with many cross-marks cut into it. It was the score pad. One notch was cut in for each sin Jancsi committed, and after a while it was crossed out. But the "after a while" usually included moments Jancsi didn't like to remember. Holding knife and stick in his hands, Father looked at Jancsi. Jancsi looked far, far ahead. Suddenly Father laughed and, putting away the "score," slapped Jancsi on the back.

"You're no worse than I was at your age, Son. You'll make a good rancher."

Jancsi heaved a sigh of relief. This was a man's world, and he was accepted!

Father pointed ahead. "See those houses and chimneys? That's the town and the station." Jancsi was all eyes and ears now. Soon the wagon was rattling on the cobbled street. They passed lots of buildings, and there were a great many people walking around. Father told him where to stop and, after the horses were hitched to a post, said: "Well done, boy!" This made Jancsi feel still better. Praises from Father were few and far between, but they were all the more satisfying.

Walking through the station building, they came to the platform. "Those long shiny snakes are rails, Son; the train travels on them. It'll be here soon now."

Jancsi heard a great rumbling, snorting, and pounding in the distance. He felt the platform shake under his feet. Casting a frightened look at his father, he saw that Father wasn't afraid, so it must be all right. Then he saw a black monster rushing around the curve. It must be the dragon. It had an immense eye glittering in the sunshine. Vicious-looking black teeth, close to the ground. And black smoke poured out of its head. Then it gave a shrill scream, blew white smoke out of its ears, and came to a groaning halt. Men jumped down, opened the doors of the funny little black houses. Jancsi waited with eyes round and shiny like big black cherries. He expected to see people in silks and velvets, glorious people. But not one of them had good clothes on; they were just everyday people dressed in drab grays and browns. Then he heard someone shouting: "Márton Nagy! Is Márton Nagy here?"

Father yelled back: "Here! Márton Nagy!" A man hurried toward them, dragging a little girl with him. Just any kind of little girl, with plain black hair, a smudgy face, and skinny legs.

"Well, thank goodness you're here," said the man, wiping his forehead. "Here, take this—this imp, this unspeakable little devil—take her and welcome." He pushed the girl to Father. "Never again in my life will I take care of girls. I'm a self-respecting railroad guard, I handle anything from baggage to canaries, but I'd rather travel with a bag of screaming monkeys than her, any time." He gave her a final push. "Here's your uncle, he'll take care of you now. G'bye and—good luck to you, Mister Nagy!"

All this tirade left Jancsi and Father speechless. Here was Kate, looking as meek as Moses, but evidently something was wrong with her. Father bent down and said: "Well, Kate, I am your Uncle Márton and this is Jancsi, your cousin. We'll take you home now."

Cousin Kate looked up. Her dirty little face broke into a grin. "Oh, but you look funny!" she cried. "And I thought my cousin was a boy, and she's nothing but a girl!"

"But, Kate," said Father, "can't you see he's a boy?"

"I only see that she has skirts on and an embroidered blouse. Nobody's wearing embroidered blouses this season, they're out of style!"

Jancsi just began to realize that this dirty, skinny little girl in the plain blue dress was his cousin. He felt cheated—that was bad enough—but she called Father "funny" and said he was a *girl*—that was really too much! With fists clenched, chin stuck out, he advanced toward Kate. "I am a girl, am I? . . . I'm funny, am I? . . . I'll show you!"

Kate was ready. She dropped her bag, took a threatening step toward Jancsi. They were face to face now, tense, poised, like two little bantam roosters, ready to settle the argument on the spot. Suddenly Father's hearty laugh broke the tension. "You two little monkeys," he cried, "now I'll tell you that you are both funny! Stop this nonsense, both of you. Jancsi! Gentlemen don't fight girls. Come on, we'll go home."

He grabbed their hands and, still laughing, walked to the baggage-room. Jancsi and Kate had no choice, they had to go, but at least they could make faces at each other behind his back. The fight was not over, it was just put off for the moment.

When they reached the wagon, there was more trouble. Kate declared that since the wagon had no top, she'd get a sunstroke. It didn't have cushions on the seat, so she'd break to pieces. She told Father to "phone" for a "taxicab."

"I'll wash your mouth out with soap, if you swear at *my* father!" cried Jancsi. "Phone" and "taxicab" sounded like swearing to him.

"She wasn't swearing, Jancsi," said Father; "she is just talking city language. 'Phone' is a little black box, you can talk into it, and people many miles away hear you. 'Taxicab' is a horseless wagon city people travel in." He turned to Kate. "We haven't any taxicabs here, Kate, so come on, hop on the seat."

Kate shook her head. "I will not. Ride in this old wagon indeed! Why, everybody will laugh at me."

Father's patience was wearing out. He just grabbed Kate under the arms and lifted her into the seat before she knew what had happened. "Come on, Son, we can't waste the whole day. You sit on the outside so she won't fall off." They both got on the wagon. Kate almost disappeared between them. Father was a very big man, and Jancsi a big husky boy for his age. But what Kate lacked in size, she made up in temper. When she realized what had happened, she turned into a miniature whirlwind. She kicked and screamed, she pinched Jancsi, she squirmed like a "bag of screaming monkeys."

"Father, the man was right, she's a bag of screaming monkeys!" said Jancsi, half angry, half amused, holding on to Kate.

Father was busy holding the horses in check. They were respectable farm horses, not used to the unpleasant sounds Kate managed to make. Soon they left the town and were traveling at a fast clip on the country road. Little by little Kate subsided. The long trip in the train and all the excitement were beginning to wear her out. She looked around. She saw the great Hungarian plain unfold before her eyes. Something in her was touched by the solemn beauty of it. Its immense grassy expanses unbroken by mountains or trees, shimmering under the spring sun. The dark blue sky, cloudless, like an inverted blue bowl. Herds of grazing sheep, like patches of snow. No sound, save the soft thud of the horses' hoofs on the white dusty road, and now and then the distant tinkle of sheep's bells, or the eerie sound of a shepherd's flute, the tilinkó. At times these plains, called the "puszta," are the very essence of timeless calm. At times the puszta wakes up and resembles an ocean in a storm. Clouds, so low it seems you can reach up and touch them, gather above. Hot winds roar over the waving grass. Frightened herds stampede, bellowing and crying. But calm or stormy, it is magnificent. Its people are truly children of the soil, they are like the puszta itself. Good-natured, calm, smiling, they, like the plain, can be aroused to violent emotions.

Kate did not know all this, but she was touched by the greatness and calm of it. She was very quiet now. Jancsi looked at her and touched Father's shoulder. They smiled at each other—she seemed asleep. Jancsi felt almost sorry for her now, she was so little and thin, so funny with her dirty little face. "Like a kitten," he thought, "the poor little kitten I found after the storm." He moved, to give her more room. She leaned heavily against him, her head nodding. He didn't see her face now, didn't see the slow impish grin, the awakening mischief in her eyes. He moved a little more, balancing on the edge of the seat. "Poor little kitten," he thought again—and "poor little kitten" suddenly gave him a hearty push which sent him off the wagon like a bag of flour. He landed in the dusty road, resembling a bag of flour indeed. He hurt something awful where he landed; it was the same spot Máli the cow had kicked that morning. Through the dust he saw the wagon come to a stop.

Father jumped down and, reaching Jancsi, began to feel his arms and legs for broken bones. "You great big baby," he scolded, "you want to ride wild horses? Can't even stay on a wagon!"

"Hey! Hey! Father! Stop Kate! Look, Father!" Jancsi yelled, struggling away from Father.

There was Kate, standing bolt upright on the seat, reins and

whip in hand. She was grinning from ear to ear.

"Pushed you off, didn't I, little girl? Catch me if you can!"
She whipped the horses, screaming at them: "Gee, git up, git
up!" This was too much for one day even for the horses. They
lunged forward, and broke into a wild gallop.

Father, shocked speechless for a moment, grabbed Jancsi
by the arm.

"Come on, Son, we've got to catch this screaming monkey
before the horses break their legs, or she breaks her neck!"

They ran, panting and choking in the hot dust. The wagon
was almost out of sight now.

"Got-to-get-horses!" panted Father.

"We-could-catch-two from the herd here!" choked Jancsi,
pointing to the herd they had passed that morning.

They jumped the fence and were among the surprised horses before the animals became alarmed.

"Run with the horse, Son," cried Father. "Run with it, grab its mane, and *swing!*"

Exciting moments followed. They were used to horses, but this was hard business, without rope or halter. Jancsi singled out a young chestnut horse. The animal reared, shied, baring his teeth, and started to run. But Jancsi's hands were already clutching his mane. The horse broke into a wild run, Jancsi clinging to him for dear life. He was carried like a piece of cloth, almost flying beside the horse. With a supreme effort he pulled himself up. Clutching his legs around the animal's neck, he reached forward to pull its nose down. Horse and rider were a mass of plunging, snorting animation. Jancsi was dizzy, but he gritted his teeth and hung on. Then he heard Father's voice through the tumult. "Let him run and guide with your knees. Come on, 'csikós,' you're a real son of mine!"

Slowly the horse quieted down. Jancsi pulled him around and headed for the fence. Father was riding a big mare, waving to him to follow. Soon they were traveling side by side— hot, dirty, exhausted, and, judging by Father's face, madder than hornets.

They rode through the village without stopping to ask questions. The poplars on the ranch road whizzed past them. There was the house now! There was Mother, at the gate, waving madly with one hand. With her other hand she was clutching the blue skirts of a dancing, struggling little imp— a dirty, disheveled, but grinning little girl—Cousin Kate from Budapest!

## CHAPTER II

### *MOTHERLESS LAMB*

WHILE Kate told her story, Jancsi cast half-amused, half-admiring glances at her. She might be just a plain little girl, but she certainly wasn't a sissy.

She was sitting in Mother's ample and protective lap, looking once more like a sleepy kitten. Father was very angry at first, but he was so relieved to see her alive, he just couldn't stay angry.

"We were going almost as fast as Ben Hur in the movies," Kate said. "Only I lost those long strings tied to the horses and then I had to sit down, I had nothing to hang on to. And the chariot was swaying so I got dizzy!" She kept on calling the wagon a "chariot." Jancsi didn't like it, it sounded almost as bad as "taxicab." "Then we came to a long street with houses. Men in petticoats, like yours, Jancsi, came running out of the houses. They were all yelling, but couldn't stop the horses. But after a while the horses got tired running, an' I was sick to my stomach anyway, so I crawled back and lay down on the straw, and went to sleep."

"The poor mite was still sleeping when I found her," said Mother. "I saw the wagon turn in at the gate without a living soul on it. The horses were heading for the stable. I ran out. There was a girl curled up in the straw! When I woke her up, she started to jabber a lot of nonsense about 'chariots' and 'Ben Hurs' and Uncle Márton and Jancsi. 'Glory be,' I said, 'are you Cousin Kate from Budapest?' I picked her up and brought her in! The very idea, leaving a delicate child alone in the wagon with four wild horses!"

"Leaving—what's this?" cried Father, but Kate broke in hurriedly: "And then we saw you and Jancsi riding like the devil was after you!"

"Only it was the other way round—*we* were riding after the devil!" said Father. "Luckily the horses had sense enough to bring you home. But listen, my girl, you are rather a wolf in sheep's clothing!"

"M-m-m," said Kate with satisfaction. "I know. That's what Father always said. Oh! He sent you a letter!" She reached down into her blouse and produced an envelop.

Father read the letter aloud:

"My dear Brother:

"I feel guilty for misleading you, so forgive me. My dear daughter Kate had the measles, and she is delicate and in need of fresh country air—all this is true. But she is more than delicate. She is the most impossible, incredible, disobedient, headstrong little imp. And she needs more than fresh air—she needs a strong hand! Pray don't let her innocent face take you in; when she looks like an angel, she's contemplating something disastrous. She is beyond me. I confess I have spoiled her since her blessed mother died. You always had a good hand with wild young things, your people always called you the Good Master, so I send Kate to you. I'll miss her terribly, but this is the best thing I can do for her.

"So forgive me, Márton, and try to put a halter on my wild colt.

> "Your loving brother,
> "Sándor."

There was a long silence. Everybody looked at Kate. She, with her eyes cast down demurely, was the very picture of innocence.

"My poor little motherless lamb," cried Mother, gathering Kate in her arms. "I don't believe a word of it. Why, look at her, Father, isn't she like an angel?"

Jancsi felt gooseflesh creeping up his spine. He had seen this angelic expression before—his uncle was right, it was a danger signal. He looked at Father and caught his eye. Father was actually winking at him. Then he stood up, and said:

"Jancsi and I are going to look after those 'wild horses,' Mother; you watch our new angel. See that she doesn't fly away."

The horses were a sorry sight indeed, caked with dust. Father and Jancsi worked hard for a long time. Under the currycomb and brush the black coats of the animals were glossy once more. After the cleaning Father gave them their rations. The stable was spick and span, the wagon put in the shed. "Time for our supper, Jancsi. Let's see what Mother is doing with the 'angel.' "

"There's Mother calling now," cried Jancsi, "but she's calling Kate."

Mother was running toward them, flushed, with all her numerous petticoats swaying around her.

"Kate! Where is Kate? Have you seen Kate? She was in the kitchen one minute, making the most awful faces at the bowl of milk I gave her for supper. Then she disappeared in thin air while I went out for water!"

They looked high and low. No Kate. No sign, no sound, of Kate. In the sheep house, the chicken coop, pigsty, cow-barn—no Kate. They looked up the roof and down the well. Back to the house, maybe she was just hiding. She wasn't in the house.

Utterly exhausted, Father sank into a kitchen chair. "If she's still alive, she's going back to the city tomorrow, so help me! I wasn't made for this sort of thing, it gives me a pain in my side," he said.

"Send the poor little motherless lamb away, Father? You couldn't," cried Mother. "Her very own father calling her names. I just know her poor little heart is broken. And you two looking at her as if she were a bug. It's enough to kill the child!"

"Tee-hee!" a sound came from the rafters. "Tee-hee!"

"Mice or rats after the sausages again. Light a candle, Jancsi," said Father. He was very fond of sausages. Mother made quantities of them in the winter. Thin long ones with lots of paprika, short fat ones with liver; she made head cheese, smoked hams. When they were ready, Father hung them on the rafters in the kitchen. He hung long rows of peppers and strings of corn on the cob. He kept bacon on one rafter, his carving tools on another. Even Jancsi wasn't allowed to touch anything stored up there.

When the candle flared up, Father was ready with a broom. Rats were his personal enemies.

"Tee-hee!" came the sound again. There sat Kate, straddling the smoky beam, skinny legs dangling, munching one end of a long sausage. Gulping down a huge mouthful, she volunteered an explanation to her thunderstruck relatives. "She gave me milk for supper. Hate milk! I like sausages!"

As long as Jancsi lived, he never forgot the uproar that followed the discovery of Kate. He wanted to laugh, but didn't dare, Father was too mad! Grasping the broom, Father roared: "Come down!" Kate shook her head. "COME DOWN!" Kate moved like lightning, out of the path of the swinging broom. Mother was wringing her hands, trying to calm Father, and

imploring Kate to come down, all at once. There was a cascade of assorted sausages, pepper, and corn. Father got red and redder in the face. Kate was scurrying like a monkey from one beam to the other, screaming like a tin whistle. It went on and on. It was Father who gave in first. He sank into his chair, wiping his forehead. "Angel . . . motherless lamb," he panted. "Look at her now. Her little heart is broken." And with utter contempt: "Delicate! Devouring yards of sausages!"

"Come down, my lamb, he won't hurt you." Mother held out her arms to Kate.

"Can't," was the laconic answer.

"How did you get up there anyway? If you went up, you can come down," growled Father.

"I climbed on that big white beehive in the corner, but it's hot now, she made a fire in it," said Kate. She meant the stove. It did look like a beehive, squatting in the corner. There was a bench around it. Jancsi loved to cuddle on the bench, propping his back against the warm side of the "kemence."

"Well, now you'll stay there until the 'beehive' cools down. Jancsi! Mother! I forbid you to take her down. She can stay there all night!" said Father. And no amount of Mother's begging and crying softened him. There she was, and there she stayed.

Mother began to serve supper. They ate in silence. Jancsi was grinning secretly. Once he looked up. Kate was peering down, her face black, her dress smoky, her stockings torn, but she grinned back.

Suddenly Father began to laugh. "Screaming monkey! Poor kitten! Colt! Motherless lamb! Why, she's a whole menagerie! You always wanted to go to a circus, Jancsi; now the circus has come to you!"

"I'm thirsty," announced Kate unexpectedly.

"Anybody would be after eating two yards of sausages. If you want a drink, come down and get it!" was Father's answer.

She tried "I'm sleepy," "I'm tired," without any satisfactory results. In fact, they were going to bed, actually leaving her perched on the rafters, and the "beehive" still too hot. She began to whimper. Jancsi felt sorry for her, but orders were orders.

Mother prepared the beds. The guest bed for Kate. This was seldom in use, all the fancy embroidered pillows were piled up to the ceiling on it. Mother carried them to a chest, put down two huge featherbeds for mattresses, and a lighter featherbed for a cover. She was shaking her head, looking at Kate, looking at Father, but he wouldn't soften. Finally they put out the candles and silence settled upon the house.

Jancsi fell asleep. The sound of soft footsteps woke him up. Then he heard whispers and a giggle. He tiptoed to the kitchen door. There was Father, holding Kate in his arms, stroking her hair.

Something made Jancsi feel all shaky inside—he felt like crying, but he was happy.

He crawled back to his bed. A little later he heard Father's voice whisper: "Good night, little screaming monkey."

Dozing off to a contented sleep, Jancsi's last thought was: "I'm glad she isn't a golden-haired princess—she's almost as good as a real boy!"

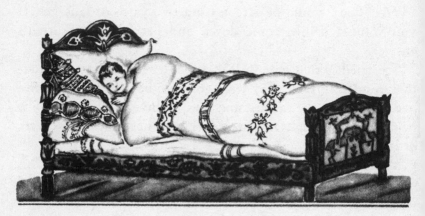

## CHAPTER III

## *THE RIDING LESSON*

Nobody ever found out just what had happened between Kate and Father that night, nobody ever spoke about it. Jancsi knew she didn't get a licking—lickings were noisy affairs. But for a few days peace and serenity reigned. Kate was left alone with Mother in the daytime. Mother never complained about her. Jancsi and Father were very busy. They had hired men to do the plowing and planting. Jancsi had full charge of the three milking cows, the pigs, and the poultry. At the crack of dawn he was up. He milked and fed the cows and strained the milk. Then he took corn and swill to the pigs, mush to

the chickens. Next he drove the ducks and geese to a grassy
inclosure with a brook running through it. On nice days he
led the cows to a small pasture close to the barn. If breakfast
wasn't ready, he helped Father in the stables. After breakfast
Father rode out to the herds. His herds were scattered over a
vast area. Horses across the river to the north, sheep to the
south. They had to be far away from each other because sheep
ruin the grass for horses, cropping it too close to the ground.
The men who took care of the herds lived in little huts close
to the corrals. Sometimes Jancsi rode along with Father. He
loved the days when he was allowed to do so. The herdsmen
were his friends; they told him stories, taught him to whittle,
to play the tilinkó, rope a wild horse, and clip sheep. Best of all
Jancsi loved the times when they were so far away from home
that Father decided to stay overnight. They cooked supper on
an open fire and ate it crouching around the embers, singing,
swapping stories, or talking about the animals. Here he was
one of the men and they never made him feel that he was just
a young boy. Later on they made bunks right out in the open
field, under the starry sky. The herdsmen had great big coats,
called "bunda." The bunda is made of sheepskin, and the
herdsmen wear it all the year round. They say it keeps them
warm in the winter, when they wear it with the furry side
in. With furry side out, it keeps them cool in the summer.
"My bunda is my house," they say, and that is true. No icy
blast penetrates it, no rain soaks through it. Jancsi loved to
snuggle down into the furry warmth of this great coat; loved
the keen smell of grass, the stir of animals close by, the song

of the nightingale, the friendly companionship of it all.

On the days when he had to stay home, life wasn't so interesting before Kate came. Chopping wood, helping Mother in the dairy, carrying water, had been his share.

The first few days after Kate's hectic arrival the relation between the cousins was rather strained. Kate couldn't get over the funny "petticoats" Jancsi was wearing. Catching her amused glances, Jancsi paid her back by gazing solemnly at the rafters, muttering something about "outlandish rats that get into people's sausages." Finally it was Kate who broke the ice. One afternoon she was waiting at the gate when Father and Jancsi returned from the day's ride. Jancsi was riding his favorite, a skittish two-year-old horse. It was dancing and prancing now, eager to get to the stable and hungry for its oats. Kate followed them and watched Jancsi unsaddle the horse and feed it.

"He's beautiful. May I pat his neck?" she asked.

"Watch out, he's ticklish," warned Jancsi.

"Takes a real boy to ride a horse like you do," said Kate with admiration, but hastened to add, "even if you do wear petticoats."

"Petticoats! Can't you see they're split?" Jancsi demonstrated, spreading his pleated pants.

"M-m-m," said Kate. "Do you think I could ride if I split my skirts?"

"I could teach you, Kate. I bet you'd make a good rider with your long legs."

"Will you, Jancsi? Honest? And then I could ride with you

and Uncle instead of messing around with old embroideries, trying to be good."

"Well . . . maybe you could. I'll teach you anyway," promised Jancsi.

Next day Father rode alone. Jancsi was working like fury, trying to finish his chores quickly. He had a surprise for Kate. There were twelve brand-new ducklings in the poultry yard. He finished his work quicker than he expected. Mother was in the vegetable patch, spading up the soil for her seedlings. He walked back to the house and called Kate. She emerged from the bedroom, walking primly and awkwardly. She looked like a very, very good little girl! The warning flashed through Jancsi's mind: "When she looks like an angel, she is contemplating something disastrous." He made up his mind to be extra careful.

He took her to the chicken coop first. He showed her the nests where the hens were sitting on eggs. Kate was bound to break some eggs to see whether there were really little chicks inside. Only his solemn promise that he would call her when the chickens began to break through saved the lives of several future chicks.

The pigsty was a total failure as an entertainment. Kate just held her nose and walked away. Then Jancsi took her to see the cows.

"Can you ride a cow?" asked Kate.

Jancsi laughed. "No, you silly, they're milk cows."

"Milk cows? Don't tell me stories, they're chocolate cows. Why, they're all brown!"

When she finally understood that you have to milk a cow to get milk, she didn't want to believe it. "Why," she said, "milk grows in bottles!" But she wasn't interested enough to argue about it—she hated milk.

The geese and ducks were more interesting to her. She giggled at the funny way the ducks waddled and shook their tails. When Jancsi finally took her to see the baby ducks, Kate clapped her hands, exclaimed over them. She was fairly dancing with joy.

"See, they're only a day old, but they can swim like nobody's business," explained Jancsi proudly. Kate wanted to pick them up, but he told her that she must never handle very young animals; they might die. Surprisingly Kate listened to him. She said: "You know what they are like? Like little bunches of dandelions, all yellow and fuzzy. Let's pick dandelions and make believe they're duckies."

When they had a heap of the fuzzy yellow flowers, they sat down on the bank and tied them into small bunches. Kate threw some of them into the brook, where they floated, looking surprisingly like the ducklings. Then something unexpected happened. The mother duck got very excited, cocked her head to one side, then the other side. She peered at these yellow bunches suspiciously. Then she began to swim toward them, quack-quacking loudly.

"Look, Kate!" exclaimed Jancsi. "She thinks the flowers are baby ducks. Oh, how funny!"

It was funny indeed. Poor mother duck called and scolded, she tried to round up her strange brood, all in vain. The

dandelions floated serenely down the brook. She got mad and pecked at one of the bunches, which promptly came to pieces. She was frantic now. She kept turning this way, that way, not knowing what had happened.

Kate and Jancsi rolled on the grass; they were weak with laughter. Then something caught Jancsi's eye. He sat up and gazed at Kate who was lying on her stomach, kicking her legs, giggling and moaning in her amusement. There was something very wrong with Kate's costume. Her dark blue skirt was spread out on both sides on the grass, but there wasn't any skirt on Kate proper, only long white bloomers. He shook her shoulder. "Kate! What—what happened to your dress?"

Kate turned her head and peered at herself. "I split my skirt because you said you'd teach me to ride," she announced calmly. She scrambled to her feet, dragging the horrified Jancsi with her. "Come on to the stable, let's start the lesson."

Jancsi was too shocked. "But, Kate, your good dress. It's ruined!"

"Phoo. Your petticoats are split and they aren't ruined," scoffed Kate.

"But you're a girl—it looks awful queer," mumbled Jancsi, trailing reluctantly after her. He wished Father would come home so he could put off the riding lesson. He picked an old fat mare for Kate. He was just puttering around with the saddles, playing for time. She watched him with interest, asking questions about saddle, harness, reins. Then Jancsi led out the horses and, casting a last hopeful glance toward the gate, gave up waiting for Father. He proceeded to show Kate how to mount. He did it first, then dismounted again, and, holding both reins, explained every move.

"Stand at the left side of the horse. Put your left hand on the pommel, your right hand on the stirrup to steady it. Step in the stirrup with your left foot and swing over the saddle." He made Kate mount and dismount several times. Then he handed her the reins, and mounted his own horse.

They started walking the horses slowly around the yard. "Please, Kate," Jancsi said, seeing her excited face and gleaming eyes, "please, Kate, don't scream. It frightens the horses. Just in case anything should happen, kick loose from the stirrups and jump."

Kate nodded her head solemnly, clinging to the pommel with both hands.

"Let go of the pommel," instructed Jancsi. "Only gypsies ride that way. Sit up straight."

"But the horse keeps bobbing up and down, and I'm so high up," complained Kate, eying the ground suspiciously.

"High up! You were higher up on the rafters," giggled Jancsi.

"They didn't bob!" was the troubled answer.

It took quite a while before Kate got used to the bobbing and learned to sit straight and loose. Then she rewarded Jancsi with a gleaming smile. "I got it. Let's go fast now."

"Not today, Kate, you'll be sore all over anyway, not being used to the saddle."

But Kate wouldn't dismount. She coaxed and begged and wheedled until Jancsi made the horses trot. This was as far as he would go, however. He stopped the horses in spite of her dark and sulky look.

"Whee-ee!" She let out a long, loud scream. Jancsi's horse immediately went into the most violent action. He turned round and round like a spinning top. He dug his hoofs in the ground, trying to throw Jancsi. He rose on his hind legs, thrashing the air viciously with his front hoofs. Jancsi clung to the plunging animal, talking to him in a soft, reassuring voice. He finally succeeded in bringing the horse to a shivering stop. Dismounting, he looked around for Kate. The incredible child sat on her old mare, watching him with great interest.

"You screaming monkey," panted Jancsi. "Just you wait till I go riding with you again. Get off that horse!"

Kate didn't seem to notice that he was mad. "Gee, Jancsi,

but you can ride! It was wonderful. This old armchair"—
pointing to her horse—"just stood here while you had all the
fun. Let me ride your horse now."

Jancsi, slightly pacified by her admiration, suddenly smiled.
"If you dismount and walk over here, I'll let you." This wasn't
a rash promise. He knew what would happen. Kate rolled off
her horse—and just crumpled on the ground.

"My legs," she cried. "I haven't any legs!"

"Come on, Kate, walk over here!" teased Jancsi.

"Don't grin at me, I can't stand up. Oooh, I hurt all over!"
moaned Kate.

"You sit there then until somebody picks you up," said
Jancsi, leaving the puzzled Kate to rub her numb legs.

He was just putting away the saddles when Father rode in.
Jancsi saw him stop and talk to Kate. He was laughing when
he came into the stable.

"How long did you keep her in the saddle, anyway?" he
asked.

Jancsi told him the story of the afternoon—except about
the split skirt. He was very uneasy about that.

On their way back to the house, Father picked Kate up and
carried her in. In the kitchen he put her on her shaking feet.
Mother, who was bending over a pot of stew, turned around
to greet them.

"Supper's ready," she started to say, but suddenly threw
up her hands. "Oh, my goodness gracious! What did you do
to the child?" The split skirt was in full evidence now. Kate,

balancing stiffly and awkwardly, was a queer sight indeed. She wasn't disturbed, however. "Had to split it to ride like Jancsi," she said.

"Split it? On purpose? Why, you look positively indecent, Kate," exclaimed Mother. "Hurry up and change your dress."

"Can't hurry and haven't any other dress!" was the calm answer.

"Well, then sit down. I'm ashamed to see such lack of modesty," cried Mother.

"Can't sit, either!" wailed Kate.

Poor Kate. She had to eat her supper, balancing on her unsteady pins, conscious of the amused glances of Father and Jancsi and the shocked looks of Mother. It was a willing and meek Kate who was carried to bed right after supper.

When Mother returned to the kitchen, Father said: "We'd better lend her Jancsi's outgrown clothes."

Jancsi approved of the idea. Mother was doubtful, but finally agreed that, Kate being what she was, she would be much better off in pants.

## CHAPTER IV

### EASTER EGGS

BUT for her long black braids anybody would have taken Kate for a lanky little boy. She was perfectly satisfied with Jancsi's old clothes. "I'd rather be a boy anyway," she said. She was always trailing after Jancsi now. Followed him from house to barn, from barn to pasture, asking a million questions. Pretty soon she began to help him. She wouldn't have anything to do with the pigs. "I like them only after they're made into sausages," she declared. But she liked to drive the geese and ducks to the brook or feed the chickens. The milking was still a mystery to her. Why anybody should go to all that trouble just to get *milk* she couldn't understand. She loved horses. Whenever Kate was missing, she could be found in the stables. Jancsi taught her to saddle, feed, and currycomb the horses. He was very proud of the way she rode. After the first painful lesson she listened to his sound advice and was rewarded one day by Father.

He looked on one day while Jancsi and Kate put the horses through all their paces. "Pretty good," he said. "Kate, the first week after Easter I'll take you with me when Jancsi and I ride out to inspect the baby lambs—providing you keep out of mischief."

She was off her horse and in Father's arms before he knew what had happened. She was hugging and kissing him until he gasped for breath.

"Uncle Márton! Oh, I'm so happy! I'll never eat your sausages again an' I'll *try* not to scream, an' I'm so glad you'll take me because—I'd have sneaked after you anyway "

"And gotten a boy's size licking for it!" laughed Father.

"Let's see, it's a whole week until Easter. Wish it wasn't so long. I don't like Easter anyway, you have to be all dressed up and nothing to do," said Kate.

"Oh, but Easter is wonderful!" cried Jancsi. "We make Easter eggs, and everybody goes visiting, there are millions of good things to eat and . . . !" Jancsi gasped for words to describe the wonders of Easter.

Kate interrupted: "Make Easter eggs? How can you make an egg?"

"Mother just dyes them, silly, and we write all kinds of flowers and patterns on them."

This was something new for Kate. She contemplated it in silence for a while. "What else do you do?" she asked.

"Go to church and sprinkle the girls an' everything. Wait and see—it's fun!"

"Sprinkle—what—sprinkle the girls!!?"

" 'Course. All the boys and young men go to all their friends who have girls to sprinkle them with water. The girls and mothers give them meat and cakes to eat and Easter eggs to take home."

"Oh! but that's silly. Slosh water on girls for no reason at all and get cakes and everything. What do the girls get for getting wet?"

"Wait a minute, Kate," laughed Father. "It does sound silly if you put it that way, but there is a beautiful reason for it. Do you want me to tell you?"

"A story?" asked Jancsi eagerly.

"No, Jancsi, the truth," said Father. "Come on, let's sit under the apple tree and I'll tell you." He spoke seriously, almost as though he were thinking aloud.

"Easter is a holiday of joy and love and giving. We welcome our friends and offer them the best we have. For us, who live on the land, Easter means the real beginning of spring—and spring for us is new hope, new life, after the long bleak winter. Spring brings warm sunshine, life-giving soft rain. Every living thing depends on sunshine and water. So we celebrate Easter by giving each other the sunshine of hospitality, and we sprinkle each other with fresh, pure water. How does your Easter greeting go, Jancsi? Say it for Kate!"

Jancsi recited:

> "My song is the song of hope,
> The voice of spring is my voice,
> All my dear friends, let us rejoice;
> God gave us sunshine, God gave us rain,
> Our prayers have not been in vain.
> Gone is the cold, cheerless winter,
> Here is glorious Easter again!"

Kate nodded. "I like it, Uncle Márton—only—I—well—I can't understand why only the girls get sprinkled."

"You can sprinkle us on Tuesday after Easter. That's when girls have a good time," laughed Jancsi, jumping up. "Come on, the horses are waiting for a rub."

The last days before Easter were busy and exciting ones. Father and Jancsi whitewashed the house inside and out. They painted the window boxes and shutters a bright blue. Jancsi and Kate selected the largest, most perfect eggs, and they were laid aside for decorating. Mother made piles and piles of nutcakes and poppyseed cakes, baking them in different shapes. Some of them looked like birds or lambs, some were crescent-shaped, some looked like stars and crosses. The cousins were always sniffing around the kitchen, waiting for "tastes."

Evenings Mother got out her dyepots and the fascinating work of making dozens and dozens of fancy Easter eggs kept the family busy. There were two ways to decorate them. The plainer ones were dyed first. When they dried,

Father and Jancsi scratched patterns on them with penknives. The fancy ones were lots of work. Mother had a tiny funnel, with melted beeswax in it. With this she drew intricate patterns on the white eggs. After the wax hardened, she dipped them in the dye. Then she scratched off the wax and there was the beautiful design left in white on the colored egg. In this way she could make the most beautifully shaded designs by covering up parts of the pattern again with wax before each dipping. The finished ones were placed in baskets and put on a shelf until Easter morning.

"I'll make some extra fancy ones for Kate. She can give them to the boys she likes best," Mother said, smiling.

"Could I try to make one or two myself?" begged Kate. "*All* by myself. I don't want anybody to see them."

"Look out, Kate, you'll get all messed up, and this dye doesn't wash off. You have to scrub it off with sand," warned Jancsi.

Kate went to a corner with her dyepots and labored for a long time in silence. When she finally put her eggs away and came back to the table, she was a sight!

"Oh, Kate, you clumsy," cried Jancsi. "Now you look like an Easter egg. Oh, you look funny." She was red paint from head to toe. Her fingers were dripping, her nose looked like a red cherry.

Jancsi's hands were wet with the dye, too, but he carefully kept his face and clothes clean.

Kate looked at him seriously.

"Jancsi, dear, there's just a little smudge of black on your nose," she said, pointing a red finger at an imaginary spot.

"Don't touch me! I'll wipe it off," cried Jancsi and, forgetting his wet hands, rubbed his nose vigorously.

"M-m-m. That's off, but your forehead is smudged, too. The smoke from the candle, I imagine," said a very sweet and solicitous Kate.

Jancsi rubbed his forehead.

"Your chin, too. My, my, these old-fashioned candles."

Jancsi rubbed his chin. Father and Mother were laughing hard, but he didn't know why.

"It's perfect now, Jancsi," smiled Kate. "Now you look like an Easter egg yourself."

"Oh, my boy," laughed Father, "won't you ever learn the ways of our sweet pussy? You are decorated for Easter all right."

Jancsi ran to the mirror. He couldn't help laughing.

"I should have known better," he admitted. "She had her angel face on. I'll tell the boys to scrub your face for you, sprinkling isn't enough."

Saturday, Mother packed all the meats, bread, and cakes in big baskets lined with snow-white napkins. They would take them to the church Sunday to be blessed by the priest. She put the finishing touches on the family's Sunday clothes. Kate didn't pay any attention to her own dress Mother had promised for Easter; she was satisfied with her boy's clothes.

On Sunday they started to dress after a very early breakfast. Kate's clothes were laid out on her bed. Suddenly a wail came from her room. "Oh, Auntie, which skirt shall I wear?"

"Which skirt? All of them, of course, it's a holiday!"

"But there are eighteen on my bed!"

"That's because you're only a little girl. I'm wearing thirty-six, but I'm a married woman," said Mother, appearing in the doorway. She completely filled it. Her pleated and starched skirts were all the colors of the rainbow, standing away from her body like a huge umbrella. She wore a white shirtwaist with puffed sleeves, a tight black vest, laced in front over red buttons. Her head was covered with a fringed, embroidered shawl, tied under her chin. She wore tight black boots with high heels. Kate gazed at her with awe.

"I'm really very young," she said meekly. "Couldn't I wear just one or two skirts?"

"All nice girls wear at least ten," was Mother's firm answer.

When Kate finally emerged from her room, she looked like a small replica of Mother. Her dress was even more colorful, with a scarlet red vest. Her sparkling, shimmering bonnet had long red and green ribbons on it, cascading almost to her knees. But Kate's face was sad. "My old boots," she said, "they look awful with this pretty dress."

"Oh, you poor lamb!" cried Mother. "We clean forgot your boots! Father! Jancsi! We forgot Kate's boots."

Father came in, solemnly shaking his head. "Hm-hm. Think of it! Our pussy hasn't any boots. What can we do? She will have to wear mine!"

He went to the cupboard. When he turned around, he held the prettiest, trimmest pair of little red boots in his hand.

"Oh," said everybody. Kate flew to him, crying: "Uncle

Márton! You are the sweetest, best, dearest uncle!" She was
trying to hug him and put her boots on at the same time.

Father left them to get the wagon while Kate was still
dancing around happily. She was kissing Mother and she even
attempted to kiss Jancsi. But he balked at that. "Only girls
kiss," he declared and stalked out after Father.

They drove to church in great state. The wagon had been
freshly painted, the horses were brushed until their coats
shone like black satin. They overtook and passed more and
more wagons as they approached the village. "Our wagon is
best of all!" said Kate proudly.

The streets around the village church were lined with ve-
hicles. The church square was packed with people. They were
dressed in brilliant colors, the women in immense skirts,
swaying, their hair-ribbons floating in the breeze. The men
all had bunches of flowers in their hats, and wore snow-white
pleated shirts and pants, and black, blue, or green sleeveless
jackets. It made the prettiest picture Kate ever had seen.
"Like a big flower garden," she whispered.

Slowly the church filled and the service began. After the
last prayer and hymn, the priest blessed the food in the church
square. Groups of friends stood around for a while, talking.
Kate was introduced to many people. Everybody had heard
about the runaway horses. She was the subject of open admiration from the village boys and girls. Here was a city girl
who not only had had the measles, but wasn't afraid of anything!

"We'll come to your house tomorrow!" promised the boys.

When Kate woke up Monday morning, Father and Jancsi had already left for the village. Mother and Kate spread the best white tablecloth on the big kitchen table and placed huge platters of meat, bread, and cakes on it. "What a beautiful tablecloth," exclaimed Kate. "I never saw anything like it in the stores."

"I made it myself, Kate, when I was your age," said Mother. "I planted the flax, reaped it, prepared it, spun the thread, and wove it into this cloth. It's more than twenty-five years old now, but it's as good as new." Kate wanted to know more about spinning and weaving, but Mother was too busy. She promised Kate to teach her all about it in the winter.

They were still arranging the baskets of eggs when the first wagon drove in. The men and boys walked in, and one of them spoke a piece:

> "Glory be to the Holy Father
> Who gave us food and pure water.
> As we water the rose to make it bloom,
> We sprinkle the rosebud in this room.
> May you live long,
> Old and young,
> Peace be with you on this holy day of Easter."

They all repeated the last line. Kate saw the flasks of water in their hands. "It won't be so bad, the bottles are very small," she thought. Just the same she squealed and ran when the boys stepped forward and began to throw water on her. There was great shouting and laughing in the kitchen. "We want eggs!

Give us some eggs, Kate, we'll stop sprinkling if you do,"
cried the boys. She ran to the baskets and gave them handfuls
of eggs. Mother invited them to eat anything they liked.
Another wagon drove in. Young men came on horseback. It
was great fun for Kate! She was pretty wet by now, but didn't
mind it. Visitors came and left; the kitchen was always full of
people and laughter. She liked the verses they spoke, she liked
the boundless hospitality, she liked ever so much to be there
and enjoy it all!

The food supply was almost exhausted when the last wagon
drove off. There weren't any more eggs. She slumped in a
chair, tired but happy.

Jancsi and Father came home in the afternoon, loaded with
eggs. "Well, Kate," asked Father, "did you give everything
away? Not one egg left for us?"

"I saved one for you and one for Jancsi," said Kate, walking to the small basket where she had hidden the eggs she had
made all by herself.

"You said I had to give the best ones to people I like best."
She smiled, holding out her hands to Father and Jancsi.

"Mine has a nice flower on it and—oooh—little ducks!
Aren't they, Kate?"

"Yes, I drew them for you because we had such a good time
with the duckies."

Father took the egg offered to him. It wasn't a very good
Easter egg, being a tiny bit smeary, but to Father it was the
most beautiful gift in the world. This is what Kate had written on it: "I like you best of all, Uncle Márton!"

## CHAPTER V

### THE TOEPINCHER

KATE opened her eyes. The May sun came through the small windowpanes, making its way between the geraniums blooming in the window box. Above, the high-beamed ceiling was still dark. She listened for a moment. There was the unmistakable sound and smell of breakfast in the making. With a sigh of relief she jumped out of bed. Today! Today she'd ride with Jancsi and Uncle Márton! She dressed in a jiffy and ran out to the yard, just pausing long enough to give a hurried hug to Mother.

Two horses were tied outside the stable. Her heart sank.

There was Father's horse, Bátor, and Jancsi's young chestnut, Bársony—but she did not see her "old armchair." Father stepped out, closing the stable door behind him.

"Where's Old Armchair? What happened? Oh, Uncle Márton, isn't it today?"

Father laughed. "Too many questions to answer on an empty stomach. I'll tell you what and where and why after breakfast. And you'll have to finish every bit of it before I tell you!" He took her hand and walked back to the house.

"Uncle Márton, I didn't scream, did I?"

"N-no."

"I didn't get into the sausages again either, did I?"

"No."

"Was it the paint I made Jancsi put on his face?"

"No."

Kate gave up. They sat down and breakfast was served. Mother put a big bowl of warm milk in front of Kate.

"Ugh! This is Jancsi's milk," she said and pushed it away. Father pushed it back.

"This is Kate's milk, and unless she drinks it she is not going to find out what happened to Old Armchair, or where or why or anything."

He sounded serious. Kate began to sip her milk with a wry face. It wasn't so terrible after all. She drank a little faster. Then she twinkled at Father. "This isn't like the milk that grows in bottles! This is almost good."

She picked up the bowl with both hands, her head fairly disappearing behind it. Father got up and walked to the door.

Over the rim of the bowl Kate's eyes followed him anxiously.

"Jancsi," he called. "Hurry up with that milky, Kate is ready for it."

"Ooooh, Uncle Márton—oh please, dear Uncle Márton, I can't drink more milky! I'll bust if I do, just look at my tummy," wailed Kate.

Father turned around. "Drink it? I don't think you could. Just look at it."

"I don't wanna look at any old milky!" grumbled Kate, holding her stomach. But she went and looked just the same. Jancsi was standing just outside the door, holding the reins of a pure white horse. The saddle and reins were studded with brass. It looked like a dream. Kate forgot her stomach, her grudge, her anxiety about the ride. She almost tiptoed to the horse and gently stroked his neck. He was real.

"Oh, he's beautiful, Uncle Márton. Does he belong to you?"

"Well, no, not any more. I sold him for a well-kept promise, an Easter egg, and a bowl of milk. His name is Milky."

"Milky?" Kate whispered. "You don't mean—oh, no, you can't mean—oh, Uncle Márton, don't tease me." There were tears in her eyes now.

Jancsi broke in in a matter-of-fact voice: "Stop acting like a girl, Kate. He isn't teasing. Come on, get on your horse and let's get going!"

Kate turned to Father, but he was half-way across the yard. He looked almost embarrassed. "We'll have to ride fast today, can't wait for Old Armchair," he called over his shoulder.

Jancsi handed the reins to the still speechless Kate. "Here, show him you can ride a good horse. You deserve it anyway." He grinned and, giving her a hearty poke in the ribs, ran after Father.

Something touched Kate's hand. Milky was nudging her with his cool nose.

"Milky. Oh, Milky!" she cried. "You are worth a million bowls of milk." She mounted and, wheeling the horse around, saw that Father and Jancsi were already far down the road. She bent low in the saddle, giving Milky a touch with her heels. They were off! Jancsi turned his head and waved.

"Come on, race you to the storm fence." They were riding abreast now, flying across the fields. Both horses were stretched out, Jancsi and Kate bent low, spurring them on. When they hurdled the fence, it was Jancsi's race, but a close one. They slowed down and turned. "That was fine, Kate," panted Jancsi. "I had to work hard to keep up with you. Look how far back Father is. He could have beaten both of us, though, if he had wanted to. Nobody can ride like Father."

"He's wonderful," said Kate with shining eyes.

"He is a prince," stated Jancsi very proudly.

Father came closer. "I'll send both of you home if you don't behave," he called. "Who ever heard of tiring out horses like this with a day's ride ahead of us?" But he was smiling. He came up beside Kate. "Thank you for Milky, Uncle Márton, he's wonderful," she said.

"You paid for it, Kate, it was a fair deal."

They rode on, talking and laughing. The sun was high when

they reached the first herd. Not a breath of air was stirring. The sheep, huddled together in great bunches, were like gray-ish white clouds rolling over the green grass. The slow tinkle of a brook was the only sound. A donkey, tethered to a post, was grazing near by. There was a small hut under the few bushes growing on the edge of the brook.

A shepherd stepped out, greeting them: "May the Lord give a good day to all of you."

"A good day to you, Pista," said Father. "How is the herd?"

"Thirty-two lambs in this bunch and no loss," said the shepherd proudly. "But they had some trouble at the Bridal Veil." He indicated the direction with his thumb.

Father turned to Jancsi. "I'll make the rounds with Pista today. You and Kate stay here."

The shepherd mounted his donkey and rode off with Father. "What did he mean—at the Bridal Veil? A wedding or something?" asked Kate while they unsaddled and tethered the horses.

"It's one of the pastures, called Bridal Veil because the wild jasmine bushes are full of white flowers in June. 'Hungry Herd,' 'Frisky Waters,' 'Singing Tree,' 'Crooked Bend'—all the pastures have names. This one has a funny name—'Toe-pincher.' "

" 'Toepincher!' " laughed Kate. "Why?"

"The brook here is full of crawfish, and if you walk in bare-footed, they surely pinch your toes."

Kate didn't know what crawfish were.

"We'll catch some for supper, but watch your fingers," said Jancsi. "Supper!" cried Kate. "I'm hungry *now!*"

"So am I. Let's eat." Jancsi walked to the saddles and produced a bundle. They sat in the shade and ate bread, cold meat, and cookies. Kate wanted to drink out of the brook. "That's no good with all the sheep around," said Jancsi. "Pista keeps spring water in gourds in his hut." They went in to look for them. The hut was just a few poles with sheepskins stretched over them. There wasn't any furniture in it, just piles of sheepskin and a bunda for a bed, and a painted chest. The water gourds were hanging on a peg.

"He makes these himself," explained Jancsi while they drank. "He cleans out the seeds and fiber when the gourds are ripe, then dries them in the sun. They keep the water fresh and cool. He makes lots of things; all shepherds do. When they come back, we'll ask him to show you his carvings. He knows stories, too, good scary ones."

Slowly they walked toward the grazing sheep. A furious, high-pitched bark greeted them. A small, furry bundle was racing toward them, yap-yapping madly. It was all long, bedraggled gray fur, without visible eyes, ears, or nose. "Here Pumi, we're friends," called Jancsi. The bundle began to wiggle and whine.

"Is this a *dog?*" asked Kate, giggling.

"The best dog there is," said Jancsi, petting the squirming Pumi. "All shepherds have one like him. These funny dogs know all there is to know about sheep. They can round up and keep a herd together, watch a herd all alone, day and night,

bring back stray lambs, keep away strange dogs. Good boy, Pumi, shake hands with Kate," he said to the dog. Pumi sat up and waved two furry paws in the air.

"Which end is he sitting on, Jancsi," cried Kate. "I can't see any eyes or teeth or anything like proper ears."

"You'd feel his teeth quick enough if you tried to do anything to the sheep. Watch him, Kate, I'll make him bring a lamb to you." He spoke to Pumi: "Pumi, bring a lamb. Lamb!"

Pumi wiggled and took himself off on his invisible feet. He circled the herd and selected a lamb. He nudged, nipped, barked, until the lamb began to run. Then he kept it on a straight course, and drove it right up to Kate and Jancsi. While they praised him and petted the frightened lamb, a sheep detached herself from the herd and came toward them, baa-baaing loudly.

"It will be the lamb's mother," said Jancsi.

The sheep came closer. There was a string around her neck, with a small ornament, like a watch charm tied to it.

"Look, the lamb has the same collar," cried Kate.

"Yes, she's the mother sure enough. Pista has hundreds of different markers, a big and a small one of each kind. When the sheep have lambs, he ties these markers on them so he can tell which lamb belongs to the mother sheep," explained Jancsi.

Pumi was restless. Something unusual was going on here; he was very uneasy about it.

"I know you don't like this, Pumi. Drive them back. Back!"

ordered Jancsi. Pumi was all animation. He had the sheep and lamb back with the herd in no time.

The heat was intense. The shimmering, sun-drenched air dazzled Kate and made her drowsy. She stretched out on the grass, blinking lazily. Then she sat up again and rubbed her eyes. She looked intently and incredulously in the distance. When they came, there weren't any buildings as far as her eyes could see. Yet now, not so far away, she saw a whole village—but it looked queer. "Why, it's upside down! Look, Jancsi, there's a village upside down," she cried, jumping to her feet.

Jancsi turned his head. "A nice one, too," he smiled.

"Let's walk over and see," cried Kate excitedly.

"Sit down, Kate. You could walk all day and all night, all your life, but you'd never reach that village! It's a mirage."

"A what? Why, it's so close I could walk over in ten minutes! There's Uncle and Pista riding through it now. Look, Jancsi, they're just— Oh, the village! It's gone! Jancsi, what is it? Am I dreaming? Tell me."

"Pista knows a real story about it, he can tell you better than I can. We'll ask him tonight," said Jancsi.

They ran to meet Father. Kate was talking as fast as she could, trying to tell him about the mirage, the crawfish, Pumi, the carvings, the gourds. She was firing questions so fast that Father held his ears.

"Hold on! Hold on, Kate," he cried. "I can see you had a good time, but now crawfish is the only thing I'm interested in. I'm hungry. You two get busy and catch some supper."

Crawfishing was exciting. They tied the round nets that Pista gave them to long rods. A piece of dried meat dangling on a long string into the middle of the nets was the bait. They held the nets well under water. Black shadows began to flit around the meat. "They're coming," whispered Jancsi. "Don't jerk the rod until you have a bunch of them inside." The net was getting heavier and heavier, the bait smaller and smaller. "Now! Jerk!" he cried, lifting the rod, swinging the full net on the grass. Kate followed and brought up another full net. The crawfish squirmed on the ground. "Look! They walk tail first, backwards." Jancsi pointed. He picked them up one by one, holding them gingerly around the middle with thumb and forefinger, and threw them into a big basket.

"Watch out, Kate," he cried, but it was too late. Kate, who was reaching with both hands into a net, straightened up screaming. She jumped up and down, trying in vain to shake the crawfish off her fingers. There were at least six big fellows dangling on her hands, holding on like grim death. Her famous tinwhistle scream brought Father and Pista running.

"The little imps, they hurt terribly," she cried.

All of them had their fingers pinched before Kate was liberated. Jancsi scolded her, Father laughed at her. Pista shook his head smilingly. "If you want rings and bracelets, little lady, I can give you better ones than these. Come with me, I'll show you."

Kate followed him, sucking her fingers, carefully side-stepping stray crawfish on the grass. "Nasty brutes," she said, scowling.

Pista opened the painted chest. "Honor me, little lady, by selecting anything you like," he said in his quaint, courteous way. There were hundreds of trinkets in the chest. Rings, chains, bracelets, little square and round boxes, carved spoons, forks, cups, salt cellars—everything under the sun. All were beautifully inlaid and painted.

Kate forgot her sore fingers. She sat down and began to examine the beautiful articles. "Do you really make these yourself?" she asked.

"All of them, little lady. Sheep-guarding leaves a lot of time on my hands, so I just keep myself occupied by whittling."

"But what are they made of? They're beautiful," cried Kate, handling a delicate necklace.

"Ram's horns, wood, bones, roots—anything I find. I make my paints from herbs and roots, too. The Lord gave us everything to use; I just find them and use them."

"But don't you sell them? They're more beautiful than any jewelry I ever saw in stores. You could make a lot of money."

"That's what I always tell him," said Father, stepping closer. "He's an artist, a great one, and doesn't know it. He should earn money and study in schools."

Pista turned to him seriously.

"What would a shepherd be doing with money, Mister Nagy? I have everything here. I am happy. Look," he said, stretching his arms wide, turning to the open doorway. "Look. The sky gives me sunshine and rain. The ground gives me food. The spring gives me water. The sheep give me shelter and clothes. The beautiful flowers, the animals, the birds, show me what to carve with my knife. Can money and schools give me better things?" He turned to Kate. "I don't sell these things for money, little lady. I give them to my friends."

"Thank you, Pista," said Kate, touched by the dignity of the shepherd and the truth of his words. "I hope we will be friends." She selected the necklace. "But I wish I could give you something in return," she said wistfully.

"Now, little lady, maybe you can! Your uncle was telling me you had schooling and know letters. Some day maybe you'd show me how to write my name. Then I could carve it on the boxes and spoons." His weatherbeaten, sunburned face shone with boyish eagerness.

"Of course I will," cried Kate. "Give me a pencil and paper."

"Those things I haven't got, but you could just draw it on the clay floor in the corner. Then I'll copy it on wood with my knife."

He gave Kate a stick and she scratched big printed letters on the clay. "P-I-S-T-A. This means Pista."

"My other name is Magyar," said the shepherd.

"M-A-G-Y-A-R," wrote Kate. "There!"

"How about teaching Jancsi to read and write, Kate?" asked Father. "I never have enough time and we can't send him to school. You know," he laughed, "you could start a school in the fall when the shepherds drive the sheep to winter quarters. Then they stay around the house all winter with

nothing to do." He was joking, but unexpectedly Kate and
Pista took up the idea with enthusiasm. Jancsi was called in
and gladly agreed.

" 'Course," he said. "Then I could read the Bible to you
and Mother."

They made plans for "Kate's school" while they built the
fire and cooked supper. They filled a large kettle with water
and hung it over the fire. When it was boiling, Jancsi dumped
in the basketful of crawfish.

"Nasty things, serves you right," mumbled Kate.

They ate supper sitting around the fire. It was getting
dark, stars began to twinkle in the sky. Kate remembered the
mirage and asked Pista to tell her the story about it.

"If you begin telling stories, Pista, we might as well stay
the night," said Father. "Let's settle down before you begin."

Pista carried out his sheepskins and his bunda. They heaped
more wood on the fire and stretched out, prepared for stories
and sleep.

# CHAPTER VI

## *THE MIRAGE*

ONCE upon a time—Pista began—maybe thousands of years ago, when fairies were still living among us, there was a village on these plains. Everything in it belonged to a very rich man. He owned the houses, the animals; even the people were his slaves. He was greedy and cruel. Always he wanted more wealth, more land, more slaves. He was so greedy he wouldn't even let children catch fish in the river; he said it was his river. The wild flowers in the fields were his flowers, nobody could pick them. If he saw a little bird pick grains or crumbs in his yard, he would kill or wound the little bird; the grains and crumbs were his! He set traps for the jack rabbits because they stole his lettuce and carrots. The people in his village were always hungry, they never had warm houses in the winter. They were clad in rags. He lived in a big house and had a hundred soldiers guard him day and night, so nobody could harm him or take anything from him. The soldiers were just as greedy and cruel as he was. Sometimes he would lead his army far away to distant towns and villages to rob and kill and plunder. The peasants lived in mortal terror of them. The soldiers rode big powerful horses, had bows and arrows and swords, and they were clad from head to toe in steel armor.

Many miles away from the rich man's village lived a poor shepherd. All he had in the world were his sheep and his little hut, but he was always willing to give food and shelter to those who came to him. If he found a hurt rabbit or bird in the fields, he would take it home with him. He could mend broken wings and crushed paws. The birds and rabbits always stayed around his hut even after they were well.

One day the rich man heard about the poor shepherd. He had thousands of sheep of his own, but he couldn't resist his greed. Early next morning he called his soldiers, and they rode out to rob the poor shepherd. They were cruel, they were greedy, but they weren't very brave. One hundred and one strong men rode out to rob one poor shepherd. They chained him to a post while they rounded up his sheep. They were hungry, so they killed a few lambs to have a feast. After the feast they planned to burn his hut, trample his little garden, and take him as a slave back to the village.

The birds and rabbits remembered the rich man. He was the one who had wounded them. They sent a nightingale to the poppyfield, where the good fairy lived, to ask her to help the poor shepherd. When the fairy heard the nightingale's story, she was very angry. She changed herself into an old woman and followed the nightingale to the shepherd's hut. The soldiers and the rich man were feasting on the lambs. The fairy went to the rich man and said: "I am very tired and hungry. Let me sit with you and share in your food."

"Ha-ha. Look at the old hag," laughed the rich man. "We worked hard for this meat. If you want to eat, you will have to pay in gold. We don't *give* anyone anything!"

The fairy said: "I am rich. I have gold. Look!"

She reached in her pocket and held out a shiny gold piece. The rich man took it greedily and threw her a little piece of meat. "Have you more gold, old woman?" he asked.

"I have lots of gold. I'm so rich all my houses are full of gold. My village is over there, beyond the poppyfield. The houses are so heavy with gold, the weight turned them upside down. I was just looking for some good strong men to turn them back again."

The soldiers looked at each other. Here was something they had missed. "We are good and strong, old woman, take us to your village," said the rich man.

"I'll do that gladly, but we can't take the horses. There is nothing for them to eat, I have only poppyfields."

"Oh, we will leave the horses here and come back for them tomorrow," said the rich man. Then he turned to the shepherd. "I'll unchain you so you can watch the horses. If any harm comes to them, we'll kill you!"

So they walked away, following the old woman. They walked and walked under the burning noonday sun. She walked faster and faster. Pretty soon they dropped their bows and arrows. "We'll pick them up tomorrow." Then they discarded their steel armor. They were getting very tired and hot, but still the old woman walked on. They came to the poppyfields. The scent of the poppies hung heavy in the air. Their heads swam. The sun dazzled their eyes. The old woman pointed ahead. "There is my village—see the houses upside down? But I am so tired—let us rest for a while."

The rich man said: "You rest, old woman, we will walk to your village and start working on your houses. Don't you worry, by the time we are through, they'll be so light they will float in the air. Ha-ha!"

They walked off, leaving the fairy behind. She lifted her arms and spoke a charm: "Follow the mirage of wealth until you perish, and may it remain there forever out of reach, to warn men against greed and cruelty!"

The rich man and his soldiers walked on and on. The village of gold seemed always just a little farther away, shimmering in the hot, still air. They stumbled on and on all afternoon, through the red poppyfields, until it grew dark. Then they threw themselves among the poppies to sleep. They never woke up again, the heavy scent of the poppies killed them all.

But the village appears, floating in the air around midday, ever since. Nobody can ever come close to it. It's just a mirage.

"Like so many things men follow blindly," said Father thoughtfully, "wealth, power, pleasure."

"What became of the poor shepherd and the horses?" asked Kate.

"Oh, when the rich man didn't come back, the shepherd drove the horses to the rich man's village. For a long time the people waited in fear for his return. Then one day a wandering gypsy told them that he had found the dead soldiers and the rich man in the poppyfields. They buried all his ill-gained treasures, divided the land among themselves, and lived happily ever after."

"That was a wonderful story," said Kate in a sleepy voice. "But," she cried then, "won't the poppies kill us if we go to sleep here?"

"No, little lady. There aren't any poppies here. Even if there were, they wouldn't kill you; they kill only bad people."

"Tell the other story now, about the Milky Way in the sky," said Jancsi.

"Not tonight, Jancsi, it's late. Besides, if you want to hear that story, ask my great-uncle Árpád. I only heard it from him."

They said good night to each other, and silence settled on the great plain. The stars winked "good night," the soft breeze whispered "sleep well," the brook gurgled "pleasant dreams." The last thing Kate heard before she slept was the incredibly sweet, soft song of a nightingale.

## CHAPTER VII

### THE ROUND UP

THE apple tree was in full bloom. White strawberry blossoms covered the edge of the pastures. The farmyard was teeming with new life. Baby chicks swarmed in the grass, pink piglets squealed in an inclosure. Máli, the cow, had a brown and white calf, marked like a chestnut. It was tottering and tumbling after Máli, getting in everybody's way. Mother's vegetable garden was coming along splendidly. The fresh green plants were standing in even rows, like so many pert little green soldiers. Swallows darted between the squatty white pillars of the porch, repairing their nest. Early one morning the stork couple came home from the south. Soon mother stork was spending all her time sitting in their nest on top of the chimney.

"The old lady is sitting on her eggs," said Mother. "It's time to start my flower garden."

Kate remembered when Mother had planted the vegetable garden. She remembered the flat wooden boxes full of tiny seedlings. She knew that the seedlings had been transplanted into the soil. Now Mother said she was planting a flower garden, but she didn't have any seedlings.

Kate watched her make furrows with a little stick, and scatter something like sand into them. She looked up at Kate. "These will be rosemaries. Now I'll put snapdragons in the next bed."

"How can you tell, Auntie?"

"Good gracious, child," exclaimed Mother, "I saved the seeds myself from last year."

Kate watched her in silence. Plant life was a mystery to her.

"Auntie! If I put some of that sand into the ground, would flowers grow for me?"

"Seeds, you mean. Of course they would. You can have a garden of your own if you want to."

Kate wanted to. Mother gave her a spade and a rake and showed her how to dig up the soil and rake it smooth. Kate worked hard. After a while she paused.

"I know, Auntie. The seeds are the eggs of the flowers, aren't they?"

Mother laughed. "I never thought of it that way, but they are."

She gave Kate little bags of seeds. Each bag had the name of the flower written on it—hollyhocks, sunflowers, bluebonnets, marigolds, carnations.

"Don't plant them deep—just so the seeds are covered."

"What next?" asked Kate when all her seeds were planted.

"We'll water them now, very carefully, so the water doesn't wash away the seeds."

"And then what?" was the next question.

"Well, we'll have to water the soil twice a day, and just wait until they grow."

When Father and Jancsi came home, Kate ran to meet them. "Uncle Márton, you know what? I laid some flower eggs today. I am going to have a garden!"

She was a very busy little person from now on. Jancsi let her take care of the whole poultry yard; then there was Milky to feed and clean and exercise. She was very conscientious about watering her garden. Every morning before sunrise, every evening after the sun went down, Mother often found her flat on her stomach, "waiting for the flowers to come up."

Days passed, sunny days, rainy days. Then one morning Kate roused the household, crying at the top of her voice: "Auntie-e-e! Uncle! Jancsi! Come quick!"

They came running from all directions, Mother from the kitchen, Father from the stables, Jancsi from the cow-barn. "Where is she? What happened?"

Kate was kneeling in her garden, waving her hands, yelling for all she was worth: "Look! Look what happened!" They looked.

The black soil she had tended so carefully showed the first promise of a future garden. Tiny seedlings, hardly visible, were pushing up bravely.

"Phoo!" cried Jancsi when he understood that he had been brought here just to look at seedlings. "A person would think that something wonderful had happened. And here you raise all this fuss for a few seedlings. Seedlings!"

"You know, Jancsi, I think something wonderful has happened," said Father thoughtfully. "It's such an everyday story to us. We know that seeds will grow into plants. But how? Why? What makes them? To Kate it's a miracle—and so it is. Look at those tiny seedlings. See how they struggle up through heavy clumps of earth to reach the light and sun. We are so used to it that we take it for granted, instead of getting on our knees to thank the Lord for another gift!"

He smiled at Kate. "Little monkey, you are teaching me a lesson, too."

"And now," he went on, "I have a surprise for all of you. I met the judge yesterday, and he told me that the big county fair will be held near our village this year—one week from today."

"Oh! And can we all go?" asked Jancsi eagerly.

"Of course we will go, but I have to get some horses for the animal show. I'm riding out to the herds across the river to round up about twenty. I want to sell some at the fair.

Jancsi, you're coming with me. And if Kate wants to leave her garden for a day, she may come along."

Kate looked at Mother. "Will the baby flowers be safe if I leave them?" she asked.

"Don't you worry, child, I'll take good care of them," said Mother, smiling.

They rode out of the yard while the morning dew was still sparkling on the grass. The north road they took today wasn't at all like the one leading to the sheep herds. There were large wheat and rye fields on both sides. Narrow paths forked out of the main road, leading to white cottages nestling under shade trees. From the distance they looked like small white mushrooms under their heavy thatched roofs. The scenery was changing gradually. There were more and more trees. They crossed many small wooden bridges, spanning brooks. Soon they could see the river Tisza, like a wide blue ribbon on the green velvet of the fields. Jancsi rode ahead. Suddenly he waved and cried: "The 'Komp' is in. Hurry, Father, they're waiting for us." They spurred their horses and clattered on to the floating ferry, the Komp. It was attached to stout ropes on both sides. The ropes stretched across the river and were wound on large wooden pulleys. There were several wagons and riders on the wide platform of the Komp.

Kate, following the example of Father and Jancsi, got off her horse and tied him to a hitching-post. "How will we get across? Row?" she asked.

"Watch these men, Kate. They'll pull the Komp across by the ropes. We can help, too," said Jancsi. A bell sounded. Another answered from across the river. Everybody walked to the ropes. "Here, Kate. Grab this rope! Pull when they say 'Hooo-ruck!' "

"Hooo-ruck!" Kate pulled for all she was worth. "Hooo-ruck!" they cried with every pull. The Komp began to move. "Hooo-ruck! Hooo-ruck!" chanted everybody, pulling and slacking. The far bank seemed to come nearer and nearer. They could see other wagons and riders waiting. There was a scraping sound when the Komp touched bottom and came to a stop. A man on the bank fastened it to a high post.

"Coming back tonight, Mister Nagy?" he asked Father when they rode past him.

"Yes, Géza, we'll bring about twenty horses. Wait for us."

The road led through a small forest of acacia trees. Their branches were heavy with clusters of white flowers. The air was drenched with their sweet, heady perfume. White petals drifted in the breeze, covering the ground like snow.

As soon as they left the forest, they saw the first corrals. They were huge grassy squares, surrounded by tall fences. Long, low stables and a few white cottages were scattered among them. Corrals and buildings formed an immense triangle. In the distance hundreds of horses were grazing placidly. Here and there a horse herder sat his horse, motionless as a statue against the blue sky. One of them saw Father and rode to him. He was an old man, but straight-shouldered and strong, with snow-white hair and a clearly modeled, sunburned face. Under bushy white eyebrows his black eyes were sharp as an eagle's.

"Welcome, Mister Nagy. We got your message. The boys are ready for the round up." He looked at Kate and Jancsi. "The young ones could stay with my wife, out of harm's way."

Father shook his head. "Jancsi is working with us this year; he is old enough to know what it's all about. But—Kate, I think you'd better stay with Árpád's wife."

"Oh, Uncle Márton, please let me go too. Please!" cried Kate.

Father looked at the old herder. Árpád shook his head. "If those horses stampede, Mister Nagy, you know what it means! A round up is no place for a girl child."

"She isn't a girl child. She's almost as good as a boy," said Jancsi stoutly. "Father, let Kate ride with me. I can take care of her."

Father hesitated for a second. Then he said: "Kate, you kept your word to me once. Will you promise me now to keep close to Jancsi and not to scream or yell no matter what happens?" He was very serious. "If these wild horses hear one of your famous screams, they'll run right off the face of the earth."

"I promise!" said Kate, looking straight into his eyes.

"Very well, you may go with Jancsi. Árpád! You take two men and start the drive from the north. Send four men to me. Two will go with Jancsi and Kate and drive from the east. I'll take two men to the west."

Even Árpád's straight back expressed his disapproval as he rode away. They saw him stop and speak to the men.

"Jancsi." Father's voice rang sharp—he was giving orders

now. "You are one of the men today. Do you know what to do?"

"Yes, Father. I ride slowly to the east fields, about two miles from here. When I pass the last herds, I turn and start the drive back to the corrals. If they stampede, I ride with them and try to take the lead to turn the herd."

"If they stampede, you take Kate out of the way and let the herders turn them. Understand?"

Then Father gave his orders to the waiting herders, and they rode off.

Kate and Jancsi followed the two young herders in silence. They rode slowly, keeping well away from the grazing horses. Kate watched the men. She wondered if they ever got off their horses or were grown to them. Straight, yet supple, their bodies followed the swinging movement of the horses in perfect, smooth rhythm.

Jancsi touched her arm and whispered: "You won't scream, Kate? Promise?" He looked worried.

"I won't make a sound, no matter what happens. Thank you for sticking up for me."

A tall split-rail fence showed in the distance. "Here's where we spread out," said one of the herders.

Kate was terribly excited. They were riding along the fence now, about fifty feet from each other. "Stampede, stampede," kept ringing in her ears. What if they stampede? But everything went well. They turned back toward the corrals. At their approach there was a ripple of movement in the herd. They stopped grazing, neighed uneasily, but weren't frightened. Slowly they began to move in the direction of the corrals. Jancsi and Kate were directly behind them, the herders slightly to the sides.

Jancsi took off his hat and wiped his forehead. His first round up was going off well and he felt very proud. The herd was moving peacefully—surely there wouldn't be any trouble. But—what was the sudden stir in front there? He stood up in the stirrups, saw a flock of partridges fly up, heard the sharp, frightened neighing of the leaders, saw the whole herd sway and swerve . . .

"They're turning! Get out of the way, Kate! Follow me!" he yelled. It was too late. The frightened herd was thundering down on them. He couldn't stop to help Kate. His own horse was caught in the panic and raced at break-neck speed. Looking around he saw Milky go like a white flash in the other direction, with Kate bent close to his neck. He yelled: "To the left, Kate!" It was useless. He could hardly hear his own voice in the deafening tumult. His own words flashed in his memory: "If they stampede, I take the lead to turn the herd!"

With a desperate struggle he pulled at the reins, his horse swerved to the right. The herd followed! "Now back to the corrals, if I can only keep ahead of them! Come on, Bársony!" He dug his heels into the horse's sides. Almost flying over the pasture, he turned his head to look for Milky. Why, the herd must have split in half! There was Kate to his far right, racing ahead of more horses than he had behind him! She was leading them to the corrals!

"What a girl!" shouted Jancsi. "Hurray!"

He was almost at the first corral gate. He checked his horse, pulling him sharply to one side. The wild horses thundered past him and raced around into the inclosure. He closed the gate quickly, just as the rest of the herd rushed into the adjoining corral. Milky, shivering and snorting, pressed close to Bársony. Kate grinned at Jancsi as she closed the gates. "Look at the herders," she said with a wink; "we beat them to it."

The two men looked rather sheepish and bewildered. There was no time for conversation, though. Father's herd came in, closely followed by old Árpád from the north. When all the horses were safely closed behind the gates, a cottage door opened and Árpád's wife came out ringing a bell. "Dinner ready," she cried.

Father turned to the silent herders. "How did my youngsters behave?"

The herders grinned sheepishly. "Behave, Mister Nagy? Behave? Why, the two of them turned the worst stampede we ever saw and brought the herd in, before we knew what happened."

"What?" cried Árpád and Father together.

"I didn't scream, Uncle Márton, did I, Jancsi?" cried Kate.

"She didn't, Father. A flock of partridges started them off. But can she ride! She rides 'most as good as you!"

"That's saying a lot, Sonny," smiled old Árpád. "Your father is the best horseman in seven counties. But tell us all about it while we eat."

They dismounted and walked to the cottage. In the doorway Árpád took off his hat. "Welcome to my house and table," he said.

"Welcome, and thank the Lord you are all here," cried his wife. "When I saw this girl child ahead of the horses, I thought we'd be picking her up in little pieces instead of sitting down to dinner! My, my, what is this world coming to! When I was her age, and a stout husky girl I was, I had to sit by the window and sew all day, and here she is, no bigger than a flea, racing with the best of you. Oh, oh, forgive my chatter, sit down and eat hearty, you must be starved!"

"Womenfolks talk more than magpies—sit down and welcome," said Árpád.

He said a prayer and a huge pot of steaming stew was set on the table.

"Now, let's hear the story," said Father when everybody was served. Jancsi laughed. "The story of a flea on horseback. She has a new name, Father. We can't call her screaming monkey any more!"

Little by little the story was pieced together. "But how did you know what to do, Kate?" asked Father.

"There was nothing else to do," she said calmly. "I remembered what Jancsi said about taking the lead if they stampeded. I didn't have to take it—they chased me!" She grinned. "Then we came to the horseyards ——"

"Corrals, Kate," interrupted Jancsi.

"Corrals, then. Anyway, I saw you pull Bársony to one side. So I did the same thing. It was easy!"

Old Árpád shook his head. "A guardian angel watched over you, child. You were in great danger."

"Maybe—maybe it was my mother," whispered Kate with sudden tears in her eyes.

There was a long silence. Father spoke then in a husky voice: "I shouldn't have let you go, Kate, but now that everything is over, I am very proud of both of you." He turned to the herders: "Ready, boys? Get your ropes. I want twenty horses, two-year-olds, the best we have."

Selecting the best of the big herd was no child's play. Jancsi and Kate watched them as they lassoed horse after horse. Their ropes swung and looped around the singled-out animals with uncanny precision. Not once did they miss the horse they wanted. It was almost dark when twenty sleek, silky horses stood haltered in the stable. Father looked them over once more.

"Faultless beasts," he said. "You are the master horse-herder, old Árpád. May you live long!"

Árpád lifted his proud old head. "Should know something about horses; all my ancestors were born to the saddle."

"How about a nice story while we rest? The youngsters would enjoy one of your tales," asked Father.

Árpád smiled. "Jancsi here knows most of them. Which one shall it be, Son?"

Kate whispered in Jancsi's ear. "Does he know the story of the Milky Way?"

"That's right. Pista told us to ask you for the story of the Milky Way. Will you please tell it?" said Jancsi.

Árpád looked at the sky. "The stars are coming out. Let's walk to the open fields; there's fresh cut hay near the well. There we can see the Milky Way from end to end."

"Don't make it too long, Árpád," said Father when they

were settled in the sweet-smelling hay. "We have to ride home tonight."

"The stars will guide you home, Mister Nagy. It's a long story, the story of all Hungarians. The Milky Way is a good enough name for other people but we call it the 'Skyway of the Warriors.' "

On the vast plains—he began—and in the mountains of far-away Asia, lived two wild, brave tribes. Huns and Magyars they were called. When their people grew so numerous that they needed more land, the Huns set out to look for a place where they could settle. After many hardships, many years, they came to a land which was green with pastures, blue with swift-flowing rivers, rich with wooded mountains. But it wasn't free land, it belonged to the Romans who called it Pannonia. The Huns were strong and bold, they wanted this beautiful land. After many cruel, terrible battles they took it from the Romans. The bravest of the Huns was a young prince, Attila, so they chose him for their king. Attila grew into a mighty monarch. He and his vast army of warriors were so feared that people called him the "Scourge of God." Attila took more and more land and ruled over his people with an iron hand. When his wife died, leaving him with two sons, Csaba and Aladár, he boldly demanded the daughter of the Roman Emperor for his wife. And not only the daughter, but half of the Roman Empire for a dowry. The Emperor refused. Attila, hurt in his immense pride, called his army and set out to conquer the Romans. But the Franks, Goths, and Burgundians came to the aid of the Roman Emperor. Huge masses of hostile warriors gathered against Attila. The two opposing armies advanced like two thundering storm-clouds. The earth shook and trembled under the hoofs of millions of horses. Forests disappeared in their wake as they built rafts and floats to cross the rivers. Finally they clashed at Katalaun. The battle was terrific and merciless. The light cavalry of the Huns swept down on the Roman army like a furious whirlwind, just to be battered to pieces on their iron-clad, massive ranks. The screams of wounded men and horses could be heard for miles. Placid rivers turned into rivers of blood, green fields were covered with thousands—no, millions—of corpses. The battle went on far into the night. Both armies were exhausted, and at the break of dawn there was mutiny on both sides. For weeks parleys went on. Terrible diseases swept through the ranks, weakening both armies. Franks, Goths, and Burgundians deserted, leaving the Romans to Attila's mercy. But the Scourge of God was broken. He ordered a retreat and led his remaining army home. Old and broken in spirit, he died shortly, leaving his army to his sons, Csaba and Aladár.

When the neighbors heard about Attila's death, they came with their armies to take revenge on the Huns. Without their powerful leader the Huns had to surrender more and more land. They lost many warriors and finally took refuge in the high mountains of Erdély. Here Csaba decided that he would take the bravest, strongest men and return to far Asia, where the Huns had left their brother tribe, the Magyars. He would bring the Magyars to help them. When he was ready to go, he called all his people together. "Dead or alive, we will return to you if you are in danger. From far-away lands we shall come to your aid if we are alive, from the starry sky we shall swoop down if we are dead," he said.

A few months passed. The Huns were attacked again by their bitter enemies. When the danger was greatest, when all hope was lost, came the thundering army of Csaba. He returned from far-away lands and saved them. Three times he returned, always when they needed him sorely. Then he was gone again. Years went by. Nobody knew where he was, whether he would ever return. A vaster army than ever marched against the Huns. Endless columns of ruthless warriors swept into their stronghold, burning their houses, killing their wives and children, threatening to destroy the whole tribe. Aladár was killed in the battle. Among the Huns there was complete disorder and great despair. Forced back to their last stronghold, they heard the mocking chant of the advancing foe. "Where is Csaba now? Why doesn't he come? Where is your brave rescuer? Where is your great leader?"

The Huns fell on their knees and prayed. Prayed for Csaba, for help, for courage to face this last battle.

Thunder, long, deep, ever-increasing thunder answered them. It grumbled and roared, deafening all with its mighty voice. There wasn't a cloud in the starry sky, but the thundering grew louder and louder. A sparkling white streak appeared among the stars, forming a great arch like a rainbow. It widened and grew so brilliant that the night became

brighter than the day. With flashing swords, the battlecry of thousands of men, the clattering hoofbeats of thousands of horses, Csaba and his warriors swept down from the sky, scattering the terror-struck enemy. Before the sky army disappeared, the Huns heard a cry: "From the starry sky we shall swoop down to save you if we are dead!"

Nobody dared to attack the Huns after this. They prospered, living peacefully and industriously. Then Csaba and his spirit army came back once more. They were leading the Magyars, to join their brothers in this beautiful land of ours. After that Csaba never came back, but the sparkling skyway, the "Skyway of the Warriors," remained there forever. If we are in great danger, if we need him, from the starry sky he shall swoop down again to help us.

When old Árpád finished the story, nobody broke the silence for a long time. They were gazing at the shimmering skyway, almost hearing the clatter of swords, the hoofbeats of horses.

"This wasn't just a story, it is history. I read about Attila and Csaba in school—they really lived," said Kate.

"They lived again tonight for all of us," said Father.

They said good night to old Árpád. Two herders were driving the horses; they were to stay with Father until after the fair. Father rode with Kate and Jancsi.

"I'll write your father, Kate," he said, "and tell him how proud I am of you."

Kate was gazing at the sky. "Can he see the Skyway of the Warriors, as we see it now?" she asked.

"I'm sure he can, Kate—why?"

"I wish—Prince Csaba would bring him home . . ." whispered Kate.

Father patted her hand. "I think he will, Kate my dear. Good wishes always come true if you say them with your face turned up—toward the sky."

A ROOSTER crowed in the yard. Another answered. It was still dark. Pale rays of the fading moon stole through the leaves of the apple tree near the house, painting a lacy pattern on the white walls. A lark trilled in the tall grass, then rose swiftly and soared into the dark blue sky, his silvery notes greeting the still invisible sun.

There was a faint stir inside the house. Jancsi woke up and

102

listened. A door creaked. Somebody whispered: "Jancsi. Jancsi, wake up!"

He slipped into his clothes hastily and tiptoed to the kitchen. He saw Kate outlined against the pale square of the open door. He followed her into the yard.

"What is it, Kate?"

"Sshh! Let's surprise Uncle Márton, Jancsi. We can get all the chores done before he wakes up. He said last night we would have to hustle this morning to get to the fair early."

"Oh, good. Wait, I'll get lanterns." He returned in a moment and they walked to the barn. "I'll milk the cows and get the water. Here's your lantern, Kate, you take care of the horses and . . ."

"I know what to do, don't talk so much." She was already running toward the stables.

They worked quietly, each noting the other's progress by the sounds of the animals. Muffled hoofbeats, a contented neigh—Kate was still in the stables. Cackle of hens, honk-honk of geese—she's in the poultry yard. The lowing of cows, grunts and eager squeals from the pigsty, proclaimed the progress of Jancsi. The sun wasn't up yet when they met at the well-house. Everything was quiet; a breathless hush came over the plains. Not a blade of grass stirred, not a sound could be heard. Even the starlings, clamoring noisily but a little while ago, were silent.

Jancsi pointed to the east. "Sunrise," he whispered. From the distant, shadowy line where earth and sky merged together, golden shafts of light rose, piercing the white mist over the plains. A few lingering stars flickered and were drowned in the brightening sky. Then slowly, majestically, the red sun rose above the horizon. It seemed to hover for a second, as if reluctant to tear itself away from the earth; then it came into full view, painting everything to the smallest seedling in Kate's garden with its glorious light. The full-throated warble of a robin rose from the apple tree, heralding the new day.

Kate sighed deeply. "Wasn't it glorious? I've never seen sunrise before."

Jancsi studied the sky. "It will be a wonderful day for the fair. Not a cloud."

"Look," cried Kate. "Smoke coming from the chimney. Auntie must be up. She will want water."

Jancsi attached the big bucket to the rope. They threw their weight against the handle on the well-wheel.

"You're getting husky, Kate," said Jancsi when all the pails were filled. "It was easy to turn the wheel today." He picked up two pails and eyed her mischievously. "But I just bet you couldn't carry two full pails."

"Who couldn't? I'll show you!" She grabbed the two remaining pails and followed him into the kitchen.

Mother and Father looked at them in astonishment.

"Where did you two come from?" asked Mother. "I thought you were still in bed."

"We just—just brought in the water," said Kate, winking at Jancsi.

"Why, Kate! These pails are bigger than you. Here, give

them to me. You rest while Jancsi and Father do the chores."

"Jump, Jancsi, it's getting late," called Father, walking to the door.

"Don't go to the stables—the horses are fed, Uncle Márton," cried Kate.

"And the cows are milked," chanted Jancsi.

"And the chickens are fed, and the pigs are fed ——"

"And the milk is in the dairy ——"

"There is *nothing* for you to do," finished Kate triumphantly.

Father looked from one to the other. He smiled. "Good farm hands earn money. You are both hired, and here is the first month's pay." He took out his purse and selected two large silver coins. "Here you are! From now on you'll both get the same every month."

It was the first money Jancsi had ever had—all his own. He held it in the palm of his hand, looking at Father with shining eyes. "How much candy will this buy, Father?"

"If you spend it all on candy, it will buy two days of tummyache," laughed Father. "Come on now, let's all help Mother, then we'll get to the fair early."

The big kitchen was a jollier place than ever, this morning. Everybody was shouting and laughing, trying to do most of the work.

Kate gulped down her milk and jumped up. "My flowers! I almost forgot to water them!" She scurried to the well-house and pulled up another bucket of water. Mother saw her as she hurried by, lugging two sprinkling cans.

"Look at the child! Running with those heavy cans! Nothing delicate about her now. Her own father wouldn't know her."

"Her own father should be here with us—he'd be happier, too," said Father seriously. "City life is not good for our kind. We belong here on the green plains; we belong to the soil and sunshine."

"Why don't you write your brother—ask him to come back home? The house is big enough for all of us," said Mother.

"I've been thinking of doing that, and I believe I will now. We can't let Kate go back to the city. Don't say anything to her about this, Son," he said to Jancsi, "we may have a surprise for her some day."

"Auntie!" Kate bustled into the room. "Did you see me carry the water? Look! See how strong I am." She rolled up her sleeve, displaying a hard, sun-burned arm. "I can lick you now, Mister Jancsi," she winked at him.

"Pooh. Nobody can lick me!" shrugged Jancsi.

"These two will run the house if we don't look out," laughed Father. "Come on, strong man, help your poor old father harness the horses."

The two herders had driven the twenty horses to the fair the day before. Now they were waiting for Father at the entrance to the show-grounds. The wagon was left with hundreds of others on a field near the village. One of the herders said: "Mister Nagy, there's a man looking at your horses. A crazy man, he wants to buy all of them!"

They found a little short, fat man jumping around, examining the horses. "Where is the man? Where is the owner?" he shouted.

"Here I am," said Father, stepping closer to him.

"Good, name your price, dear sir, name your price. I want these horses, and I'm in a hurry!"

"You never make a good deal in a hurry," said Father calmly. Then he named his price.

The man looked at him, reaching for his wallet. "I want your herders to drive them to the train. How much for that?"

"You settle that with the boys," said Father.

The deal was completed in a few minutes. The little man smiled shrewdly. "You're a fool, Mister, I would have given you twice as much. Best horses in the show!"

"You would have been a fool if you would have paid more. It was the fair price—that's all I wanted," said Father.

"Oh, what luck!" cried Jancsi. "Now you can stay with us all day, Father."

"So I can, Son. And because we had such good luck, I'll buy each of you something you want most. We'll look at everything first; then you can tell me what you want."

Early as it was, the fair was in full swing. From near and far people had gathered to make the most of the event. A whole city of tents and booths had sprung up overnight. Thousands of people thronged the alleys between the booths, buying and selling, shouting and laughing. Worries about crops and animals were forgotten. It was the day of days— the County Fair. Gypsy music, singing, shepherds, flutes, tin horns, drums, whistles and trumpets, hoarse cries of dealers, laughter, the neighing and bellowing from the cattle show— the glorious, happy din could be heard for miles.

They walked up and down between the booths. Kate and Jancsi jumped and ran from one booth to another—there was so much to see! Gayly decorated whips and shepherd's canes, sidebags to sling over your shoulder, flutes and bagpipes, hats, boots, shawls, blouses, jingling spurs, big white sheepskin coats with wonderful ornaments embroidered on the smooth side— all and everything in the most brilliant colors. Farther down they came to the potters' tents. Long rows of red, blue, yellow, green dishes, sewers, cups, mugs—amusing figures, flowers, animals painted on all of them. The woodcarvers came next—chairs, cupboards, candlesticks, spoons, dippers, props for potted flowers, statues, picture frames, toys, candles, dolls —on the shelves, on the floor—carved and painted and polished until every article shone like a jewel. It was a riot of color. And everywhere happy, laughing people, jostling and joking, loaded with bundles.

When they finally came to the last booth in the last row, the four of them looked as if they had been through a hurricane. Jancsi had lost his hat, Kate's black hair was all over her face, Mother's neat shawl was hanging down her back, and even Father's face had a black smudge on it. He laughed. "Can you remember what you wanted to buy?"

"I know what I want," declared Mother, wiping her hot face. "I want to sit down somewhere in the shade and have a bite to eat."

"Wisely spoken, Mother. Let's walk to the big tent."

Inside the tent it was cool and shady. Long narrow tables had been set up. People were crowded around them but willingly made room for the newcomers. When Father asked Jancsi what he wanted to eat, even the man who waited on them laughed. Because Jancsi ordered: "A big piece of chocolate cake with a pink coat, a mug of chocolate with a white hat on it, and a bottle of that green drink," pointing to the rows of soda pop on the counter.

"Bound to get a tummyache, aren't you, Son? Well, the fair comes only once a year."

While they were eating a gypsy band came in. Whoops and hurrahs greeted them. Grinning as only gypsies can, they started to play. They played sad tunes, lively tunes, swaying with the rhythm of their own music. People began to sing. Young men jumped up, one after the other—they threw money to the swarthy leader, ordering songs for their friends, best girls, mothers. Jancsi watched them, his face eager. Suddenly his eyes sparkled. "Father! Will my money buy a tune from the gypsies?"

"Just about one tune!"

"What is your song, Mother?" asked Jancsi.

"My song? Why—a csárdás," said Mother.

Jancsi got up, threw back his shoulders, hitched up his belt, and walked to the leader. He threw his silver coin on the floor, like the other men. "Here! Play a csárdás for my mother," he ordered in a loud voice.

Cheers and applause greeted him. "May you live long, little

bantam." "Hurray!" people cried. One old shepherd held out
his hand. "Shake hands, boy. You are a true son of the plains."

Jancsi strutted back to the table. The leader followed him,
playing his violin, bending close to Mother. She listened with
shining eyes.

Kate tapped her heels on the floor to the rhythm of the
lively csárdás. "Can you dance, Jancsi?" she asked.

" 'Course I can dance the csárdás. Want to?" He held out
his hands to her. They began to dance.

"Hurray! Good for you, Son," people applauded. The
gypsies played faster and faster. Other couples joined the
dance—they pushed the tables aside. Soon everybody was
dancing, even Father and Mother. Outside the tent people
stopped, then, carried away by the irresistible tempo of the
csárdás, joined the dance. More and more coins clinked to the
gypsies' feet, faster and faster they played. "Yoo-hoo! Faster,
gypsy, faster! We live for today!" shouted somebody. The
dance was getting wild.

Father tapped the swirling Jancsi on the shoulder. "Come
on, Son, let's get out of here."

They left and walked slowly toward the booths again.
Father wiped his face. It was awfully hot. "You young swain,"
he smiled at Jancsi, "spending a month's pay on a tune. I'm
glad we are out of there—there will be a fight before they are
through."

"I haven't had such a good dance since our wedding day,"
said Mother, trying to straighten her dress and hair. "Thank
you, Jancsi, it was wonderful."

"Oh, look," cried Kate. "What are those hearts?" She ran
to a tent full of honeycakes. They were made in many shapes,
flowers, animals, houses, but most of them were heart-shaped,
with red icing. There were little flowers and ornaments on
them, made of many-colored candy, even little sayings
written in white icing. The young men and girls give them
to each other—the Valentines of Hungary.

"Ooh! They are pretty!" cried Kate. "Look at this big one
with the little round mirror set in it. And a saying, too!
Listen, Jancsi:

> " 'You may be plain
> And sometimes even silly,
> But you are the only girl for me!' "

Jancsi laughed. "I'll buy it for you, Kate," he said proudly,
reaching for his money. Oh! He blushed—and stole a quick
glance at Father. He saw Father wink at him, and felt a coin
pressed into his hand. Nobody saw it! Jancsi winked back—
after all this was something between *men!*

"Thank you, Jancsi," said Kate, hugging the big honeycake
heart happily. "I never had anything as pretty as this! Now I
want to buy something for you."

The next booth was full of pocketknives, whistles, whips,
spurs. Jancsi's eyes shone. He handled everything, couldn't
tear himself away.

Father said: "Remember, each of you can have one gift
from me—anything you want!"

"A pair of spurs," cried Kate. "May I have a pair of jingly
spurs?"

"A *girl* with *spurs!*" exclaimed Mother, shaking her head. But Kate got her spurs, the pair with the loudest jingle.

"Me, too," decided Jancsi, who was wavering between a pocketknife and spurs. He was still looking at the knife, however, opening and closing its many blades. Finally he put it down with a sigh. *One* gift, Father had said.

"Mister," called Kate to the man behind the counter. "Will this money buy that knife?" She held up her silver coin.

"It'll buy two knives, little lady."

"It will? Here, give me two, exactly the same." She handed one to the bright-eyed Jancsi. "Now we can carve like Pista."

"Mother, it's your turn now," smiled Father. "And remember, nothing for the house, nothing for me or the children. This gift has to be something for yourself. We'll get all the other things we need later on."

"I would—I *would* like some—scented soap," admitted Mother, smiling almost bashfully.

"Scented soap it will be then, my best girl," said Father. It turned out to be a whole big box of soap, every piece a different color, and a different delicious smell. Then they bought dishes, groceries, hardware, shoes, clothes, everything they couldn't make at home, enough to last until next year. Staggering under bundles, they made their way back to the wagon.

"Are we going home now?" asked Kate.

"Not yet. Listen!" said Father.

The squeaky tones of a hand-organ sounded in the distance. People were running in that direction. "The circus! The circus is here!"

"Whee!" came Kate's best tinwhistle scream. "Whee!"

Jancsi tugged at Father's coat sleeve. "A *real* circus with funny men and everything you told me about?" he asked with shining eyes.

"I think so. We'll see."

Following the crowd, they came to an immense tent, set up outside the village.

"Ladie-e-e-s and gentlemen!" howled the barker. "Come in and see—the seven wonders of the world! The biggest show ever! Trained seals—all kinds of freaks—the bearded lady—the man from Mars—hair-raising acrobatics—lions—tigers —elephants—trained fleas—man-eating sharks—and the only existing miracle of miracles— the bee-uuu-tiful, marvelous girl, a girl without a body! Just a head, ladies and gentlemen —a living, talking, smiling head—and no body at all—at all! Come in and see—only ten coppers admission!"

From the minute the show began until the very last moment, Jancsi sat spellbound. This was better than fairy stories. The spangled, glittering costumes, the prancing horses actually dancing to tunes, the lumbering elephants with people sitting on them who must be kings because they wore such marvelous rich gowns. Then the seals balancing big balls on their funny stub noses, the monkeys so much like ugly little men. He was speechless with wonder. The antics of the clowns set him howling with laughter.

When the band played the final march, he didn't want to leave. "Come on, silly," said Kate, "we can see the side-show now, with the freaks." She felt very wise and experienced now. She had seen all this before with her father in Budapest.

Here were more things to astonish Jancsi. Everything was true and real to him. He believed every single word the guide said. So did the rest of the country folk. There were gasps of astonishment and cries of surprise. There was a big crowd around the glass cage with the head of a blond girl in it. She was smiling and talking—and anybody could see it was only a head—why, you could see through the glass cage—there wasn't anything in it!

"Poor little lass, isn't she pretty—and she has no arms or legs or anything," sighed a fat peasant woman, tears rolling down her cheeks.

Kate tugged at her apron. "Don't cry, it's a fake," she whispered. "My father told me—it's just a fake! She is really a girl like anybody else."

"Sshh! Don't you fib, Kate, you can *see* she hasn't any body at all, just propped up on the glass, she is," grumbled Jancsi.

"Fib! I tell you she has arms and legs. My father said she has—it's all done with mirrors, he said."

"I don't believe it. The man said she hasn't, so she hasn't!" stated Jancsi, as a final argument. The man had a red coat and blue breeches with gold buttons and braid—he had a nice loud voice—why, he couldn't play tricks.

"You don't believe my father?! I'll show you!" cried Kate. She slipped out of reach and out of sight, disappearing behind the immense skirts of the women.

Jancsi looked around in alarm. He was surrounded by strange people, packed in around him, pressing him close to the rope that separated the glass cage from the crowd. Father was far behind other people. Jancsi couldn't talk to him. He turned around again to look for Kate. She was up to something—but how to find her? He cast another glance at the smiling head—the smile disappeared—the girl screamed. There was a clink of glass—the front of the glass cage moved and fell to the ground, breaking to pieces. A murmur of amazement ran through the crowd, changing into a howl of laughter.

"Kate!" yelled Jancsi. Grinning triumphantly, the impish face of Kate appeared from behind a pair of perfectly normal legs, clad in riding breeches and boots—very evidently belonging to the poor girl without a body.

"Take her away, she's pinching me!" screamed the girl.

The guide jumped across the rope and grabbed Kate. "I'll give you a licking! I'll send you to jail for this!" he cried, shaking her.

But the crowd was all for Kate. "Hey! Let go of that child. Let go of her! We'll send *you* to jail! Tricks, cheats, blackguards. We'll wreck your whole show!" They felt foolish and cheated and they looked dangerous.

"But my mirror! Who will pay for my mirror?" wailed the man.

Kate wriggled and tore herself loose from his hands. "I told you she was a fake!" she cried, slipping under the rope.

Father elbowed his way through the milling crowd, taking triumphant Kate and amazed Jancsi by the hand. He pulled them through the crowd, and they hurried out of the tent.

Jancsi looked at him. O-o-oh! His face didn't promise anything good for Kate. He didn't say a word until they reached the wagon.

Kate was getting uneasy. "My father told me how it was done! Jancsi didn't believe it! Uncle Márton, don't be angry, please! It *was* a fake."

Father set her on the wagon. "Listen to me, now. Fake or no fake, this is going a little too far!" He was scowling, holding the wiggling Kate firmly by her shoulders. "You know what you deserve?"

Kate nodded, blinking back her tears. Then she reached out and touched his cheek with one finger. "But the man *lied!* It *was* a trick!" she whispered. Father scowled harder, but his mouth began to quiver. Kate saw it and her own face crinkled into a timid little grin. Jancsi giggled, she was so funny. Mother began to laugh.

Father tried very hard to scowl, but he burst out laughing instead—it was too much for him. He lifted Kate off the seat and, hugging her to him for a second, set her on the ground. "You! You incredible child!" he gasped. "That man fooled me, too! Big bumpkin I am, he fooled me!"

"You won't spank me, Uncle Márton?"

"N-no. Not now! I can't, when I think of your dirty little face grinning at me from that cage. You are a circus *and* a side-show, but you aren't a fake—you're genuine!"

"Oh, but I'm tired," sighed Mother. "Let us go home—we have had a wonderful day."

"A wonderful day! Thank you, Father," mumbled Jancsi,

curling up in the straw next to Kate. As the wagon rolled home in the moonlight, Kate, Jancsi, and Mother were fast asleep.

"A wonderful day," sighed Father. "Thank You for all Your blessings," he whispered, looking up toward the moonlit sky.

# CHAPTER IX

## STRANGE WATERS

THE yellow ducklings and fuzzy, lemon-colored chickens had lost their fluffy down. Now they were gawky, awkward little creatures. Real new feathers were growing slowly, giving them a very untidy appearance. Kate's garden was full of sturdy green plants, some of them even had buds. Mother found fresh string beans and peas and picked a whole basketful one morning. There were many small green apples on the tree, pulling down the branches until Father propped them up with long sticks. Rabbits played in the cornfield. They were as saucy and fresh as only rabbits can be, knowing per-

119

haps that the corn was high enough now to hide them safely. Kate loved to sit near the edge of the field waiting for the little rascals to venture out. She would be quieter than a mouse, watching the amusing hop, skip, and jump of baby rabbits. Mother and Father called them pests and nuisances because they ate fresh lettuce and radishes. But Kate loved them.

"They can have my share," she said.

Long-necked young storks clamored in their nest on the chimney; baby swallows cried for more and more food, keeping the old swallows busy all day. The summer wore on. In the daytime it was blindingly, cruelly hot; the nights were sultry. Only the house, with its two-foot-thick walls and wide shady porches, stayed cool. For weeks it had not rained. The earth was dry and cracked; the brook dried up, leaving only a wide clay bed full of cracks with a small trickle of muddy water in the middle of it. To keep the flower gardens well watered was hard work now, and even Kate's strong, sturdy little back ached sometimes. Mother gave up trying to water her flowers. She had enough to do to keep the vegetables from wilting. Kate took care of her flowers, too, as she couldn't bear to see them go thirsty, drooping sadly toward the ground.

Father was beginning to look very worried. If rain did not come soon, wheat and rye would go to waste, pastures would dry up, leaving the animals hungry. He didn't take Jancsi and Kate with him now when he was riding.

"You two stay here and help Mother—it's very hard for her these hot days."

Even the sunrise wasn't beautiful now. The sun came up orange-colored, sultry, flooding the parched countryside with heat—more heat. In church the priest prayed for rain. People came out after services, just to see the same unbroken, bluish-white, blazing sky above—and went home dejectedly. Hot winds drove clouds of loose dirt over everything, leaving the plains under a blanket of choking white dust.

One evening the family gathered on the porch. It had been the hottest day yet. Even the well was drying up. Father sat stooped forward, his elbows on his knees, head buried in his hands.

"If this drought does not break, I am ruined," he said in a low voice.

Kate and Jancsi were whispering in the corner. They came forward now. Jancsi touched Father on the shoulder. "Father!"

"What is it, Son?"

"We, Kate and I, have been thinking. Please don't worry so, Father. Look! We'll help you—here is the money you gave us for this month."

Father held out his hands, but he didn't take the money. He pulled Kate and Jancsi very close to him. He smiled for the first time in weeks, a happy smile. "Thank you, children," he said. "I don't think I'll need the money just now, but I thank you. You have helped me—more than you know! I won't worry any more. As long as I have you and Mother, I have the greatest gifts life can give a man."

He turned to Mother. "We won't worry any more, Mother. Tell us one of your funny stories now, before we go to bed."

"A very funny one, Mother, please, to make Father laugh," said Jancsi.

"Well, then—I'll tell you the story of the Little Rooster and the Turkish Sultan."

Somewhere, some place, beyond the Seven Seas, there lived a poor old woman. The poor old woman had a Little Rooster. One day the Little Rooster walked out of the yard to look for strange bugs and worms. All the bugs and worms in the yard were his friends—he was hungry, but he could not eat his friends! So he walked out to the road. He scratched and he scratched. He scratched out a Diamond Button. Of all things, a Diamond Button! The Button twinkled at him. "Pick me up, Little Rooster, and take me to your old mistress. She likes Diamond Buttons."

"Cock-a-doodle-doo. I'll pick you up and take you to my poor old mistress!"

So he picked up the Button. Just then the Turkish Sultan walked by. The Turkish Sultan was very, very fat. Three fat servants walked behind him, carrying the wide, wide bag of the Turkish Sultan's trousers. He saw the Little Rooster with the Diamond Button.

"Little Rooster, give me your Diamond Button."

"No, indeed, I won't. I am going to give it to my poor old mistress. She likes Diamond Buttons."

But the Turkish Sultan liked Diamond Buttons, too. Besides, he could not take "no" for an answer. He turned to his three fat servants.

"Catch the Little Rooster and take the Diamond Button from him."

The three fat servants dropped the wide, wide bag of the Turkish Sultan's trousers, caught the Little Rooster, and took the Diamond Button away from him. The Turkish Sultan took the Diamond Button home with him and put it in his treasure chamber.

The Little Rooster was very angry. He went to the palace of the Turkish Sultan, perched on the window, and cried:

"Cock-a-doodle-doo! Turkish Sultan, give me back my Diamond Button."

The Turkish Sultan did not like this, so he walked into another room.

The Little Rooster perched on the window of another room and cried: "Cock-a-doodle-doo! Turkish Sultan, give me back my Diamond Button."

The Turkish Sultan was mad. He called his three fat servants.

"Catch the Little Rooster. Throw him into the well, let him drown!"

The three fat servants caught the Little Rooster and threw him into the well. But the Little Rooster cried: "Come, my empty stomach, come, my empty stomach, drink up all the water."

His empty stomach drank up all the water.

Little Rooster flew back to the window and cried: "Cock-a-doodle-doo! Turkish Sultan, give me back my Diamond Button."

The Turkish Sultan was madder than before. He called his three fat servants.

"Catch the Little Rooster and throw him into the fire. Let him burn!"

The three fat servants caught the Little Rooster and threw him into the fire.

But the Little Rooster cried: "Come, my full stomach, let out all the water to put out all the fire."

His full stomach let out all the water. It put out all the fire.

He flew back to the window again and cried: "Cock-a-doodle-doo! Turkish Sultan, give me back my Diamond Button."

The Turkish Sultan was madder than ever. He called his three fat servants.

"Catch the Little Rooster, throw him into a beehive, and let the bees sting him."

The three fat servants caught the Little Rooster and threw him into a beehive. But the Little Rooster cried: "Come, my empty stomach, come, my empty stomach, eat up all the bees."

His empty stomach ate up all the bees.

He flew back to the window again and cried: "Cock-a-doodle-doo! Turkish Sultan, give me back my Diamond Button."

The Turkish Sultan was so mad he didn't know what to do. He called his three fat servants.

"What shall I do with the Little Rooster?"

The first fat servant said: "Hang him on the flagpole!"

The second fat servant said: "Cut his head off!"

The third fat servant said: "*Sit* on him!"

The Turkish Sultan cried: "That's it! I'll sit on him! Catch the Little Rooster and bring him to me!"

The three fat servants caught the Little Rooster and brought him to the Turkish Sultan. The Turkish Sultan opened the wide, wide bag of his trousers and put the Little Rooster in. Then he sat on him.

But the Little Rooster cried: "Come, my full stomach, let out all the bees to sting the Turkish Sultan."

His full stomach let out all the bees.

And did they sting the Turkish Sultan?

THEY DID!!

The Turkish Sultan jumped up in the air.

"Ouch! Ouch! Ow! Ow!" he cried. "Take this Little Rooster to my treasure chamber and let him find his confounded Diamond Button!"

The three fat servants took the Little Rooster to the treasure chamber.

"Find your confounded Diamond Button!" they said and left him.

But the Little Rooster cried: "Come, my empty stomach, come, my empty stomach, eat up all the money."

His empty stomach ate up all the money in the Turkish Sultan's treasure chamber.

Then the Little Rooster waddled home as fast as he could and gave all the money to his poor old mistress. Then he went out into the yard to tell his friends, the bugs and worms, about the Turkish Sultan and the Diamond Button.

"Oh, oh," giggled Kate, "tell us another funny story, Auntie, please!"

"Wait!" said Jancsi. "I think I heard something just now. It sounded like thunder."

"It *is* thunder!" cried Father, as another low rumble came.

They jumped up and ran out to the yard. Heavy clouds were gathering above, blotting out the stars. The leaves of the apple tree began to whisper as the wind came up. The thunder grew louder; there was a crash of lightning. A gust of moist, cool wind whipped dust and stray leaves high in the air, bringing the fresh smell of rain with it.

"A storm! It will rain, Father, it will rain!" cried Jancsi. "Oh, please let it rain," he whispered then, looking at the lowering clouds. A heavy, big drop fell on his upturned face. "Rain! It *does* rain!"

The storm was upon them in a minute. The branches of the apple tree creaked and swayed in the howling wind. More and more drops fell, leaving big round holes on the dusty ground. Flashes of lightning came so fast it was almost as bright as daylight. Thunder roared continuously, shaking the very ground.

"Rain! Come, rain!" cried Jancsi, bracing himself against the heavy wind. And the rain came. It came down in sheets, torrents of cool, fresh rain. They were soaked to the skin but didn't think of going inside. Father stood very still, his face turned to the clouds, his outstretched arms welcoming the storm.

Mother was the first one to think of common sense. She sneezed, once, twice. "My goodness! Just look at the four of us, great big sillies we are! Come in, children; come in, Father. It will keep on raining now without your catching your death of cold."

"Ker-choo," came a sneeze from Kate.

"There you go! Inside with you—quick, now."

"Oooh! I *am* wet," cried Jancsi, shaking himself like a puppy, splattering water all over the kitchen. As they walked, their boots made clucking little noises, leaving rivulets of water on the floor.

"Indeed we are wet! The very idea! Hurry up, put some dry clothes on—all of you. Yes, you too, Father, you great big baby. Go on, now, no back-talk," she laughed as he shook his head. "I'll have to be the one to nurse you if you come down with a cold. And I'll make some hot milk and honey as soon as I get into something dry."

They came back to the kitchen, carrying wet clothes. "Just throw those things on the porch," directed Mother. "I'll wash them tomorrow. We'll have water now, thank the Lord!"

The storm passed, but the rain didn't stop. It poured down steadily, making a silky, whispering sound. The keen, fresh smell of wet earth came in through the open door.

Mother spread the table with the gayest red-and-white checked cloth. She lighted three candles and took the new flowery mugs off the shelf.

Kate clapped her hands. "It looks like a party!"

They drank the hot milk and honey, and went to sleep later to the lullaby of distant thunder and the gurgle of water in the swelling brook.

It rained for three whole days. When the sun came out again, every leaf, every blade of grass, was a freshly washed, glistening, emerald green. Little pink and yellow buds peeked out of their tight green coats, promising to burst into bloom any minute. Wild strawberries were so plentiful. Kate and Jancsi could eat all they wanted without moving from one spot. Mother made jam and preserves, storing the jars in the dairy.

One morning Father asked: "Can you spare the 'farm hands' for a day, Mother? I'm riding to the river to see the wheatfields."

The "farm hands" knew Mother. They didn't wait for her answer, but were already galloping toward the stables. They came back leading the three horses.

Kate called to Mother: "Listen, Auntie!" She knocked her heels together; there was a loud jingle. "Hear my spurs? Jancsi has his on, too. Jingle them, Jancsi." They walked up and down on the porch. Jingle—jingle—jingle, went the spurs.

"What will we do today, Uncle Márton?" asked Kate on the way.

"There won't be much for you two to do, unless you want to stay in the saddle all day. I thought I would leave you and Jancsi by the river, near the ferry, you know, because I'll have to ride from one field to the other. It's all pretty much the same. Just look at fields of wheat and rye and talk about labor, harvest, weeds, bugs, and such things. What do you think?"

"Could we ride back and forth on the ferry?" asked Kate eagerly.

"You could do that. I'll ask Géza to let you ride all you want."

Father went over with them to the other side of the river and talked to Géza. Then they came back together on the Komp. "I'll be back by sundown," said Father and rode off.

Riding back and forth on the Komp was fun for a while, but the novelty soon wore off.

"Let's stay with Géza and talk to him," proposed Jancsi.

"Tell you what," cried Kate. "Let's go swimming."

"Can you swim, Kate?"

"Swim and dive, too. I can stay under water for the longest time. Can you?"

"N-no," admitted Jancsi. "I can splash around, but I can't swim. My horse can, though," he added proudly. "He swims like a fish."

"Well, you can watch me then or—maybe I could teach you," offered Kate.

"Maybe. I'll bring the horses down to the water. They like to go in," said Jancsi. He walked to the horses and led them to the river's edge. Kate slipped off her clothes and boots, then ran into the shallow water.

"Come in, Jancsi, it isn't deep. And it's just *so* nice and warm."

Jancsi tugged at his boots, watching Kate enviously. She went farther and farther in, then she began to swim. He rolled up his pants and unbuttoned his shirt. Kate disappeared! Jancsi looked up and down; he began to get frightened. Then Kate bobbed up, almost in the middle of the river. "Oh! It's real deep out here, I can't touch bottom," she cried.

"Come back, Kate. Don't go farther in, the current is awful strong," yelled Jancsi. He was very uneasy about this swimming business anyway. They hadn't asked Father.

Kate laughed. "Sissy!" and dove under water again. When she came up, she was still farther out where the strong current made a crest on the water. It tore her away, carrying her swiftly downstream.

"Hey!" she cried once, then: "Help! *Help!* It's taking me away."

Jancsi was desperate. He shouted to the approaching Komp, he saw men pointing to Kate. They saw her, too! But they'd never reach her.

A thought struck him and he was on his horse like lightning. "Come on, Bársony."

Bársony plunged and began to swim powerfully toward Kate. The current caught him, too, but he was steady. Jancsi clung to him, watching Kate's bobbing head.

"I'm coming, Kate," he shouted. He was gaining fast. Now

he could see her pale face and frightened eyes. When Bársony was close to Kate, Jancsi reached out and grabbed her hair. She clung to his arm, almost pulling him off the horse.

"Grab my leg and pull up, Kate." He helped her scramble up behind him and felt her arms clutch his waist. He turned his attention to the horse, pulling its head toward shore. "Good old Bársony."

The horse was exerting all his strength to get free of the current. Soon they were swimming in quiet water, then wading up the shallow shore. Men came running. There was Géza, looking as white as a sheet.

Jancsi stopped the horse and helped Kate off. She was still very pale and trembled like a leaf. She managed a wan smile. "Thank you, Jancsi," she stuttered. "I—didn't—know—a current could be so strong!"

People were all around them now. Géza threw his coat around Kate. "What will Mister Nagy say? He told me to keep an eye on you. What will he say?"

A man clapped Jancsi on the shoulder. "Great work, Son, you saved the girl's life."

"He's my cousin," said Kate proudly, in spite of her chattering teeth.

Long after the other men went on their way and Kate was dressed and her own self again, poor Géza lamented: "What will Mister Nagy say?" Then he turned to them hopefully. "Do we *have* to tell him? Your clothes are dry, there is nothing to give you away."

Kate was watching the road all this time, thinking the same

thing: "What will he say?" and mostly: "What will he do?"
Now she shook her head. "I guess we'll have to tell him," she
sighed.

Father came just before sundown.

"Well, children, did you have a good time?" Nobody answered. Géza had deserted them, taking his worries across
the river just before Father arrived.

"Well—what happened? Kate, you are as pale as a ghost.
And you, Jancsi. What in the world is the matter with you?"

Kate took a deep, deep breath.

"I went swimming and got into the current and almost
drowned and Jancsi came after me on Bársony and he saved
me and it was my fault!" She managed to blurt out everything before she lost her courage.

Father looked at them seriously. "Tell me just how it
happened."

They told him everything. Kate finished the story. "Jancsi
saved me—the man said so, too. He said: 'Great work, Son,
you saved the girl's life.' I told them he is my cousin!"

Jancsi stepped forward. "Don't be angry, Father. She can
swim like anything, but she didn't know about the current."

"I am not angry, Son. I am thankful that nothing serious
happened to Kate and I am proud of you. She was foolish
to venture into strange water alone, no matter how well she
can swim. But from now on you'll know better, won't you,
Kate?"

She nodded her head solemnly.

"Well, then, let's go home. And mind, not a word about this to Mother. She would put both of you to bed for a week!" He laughed. "Come on, rascals, get on your horses."

Kate turned to Jancsi and whispered: "He won't spank me?"

"*Naw!* He never does unless you're just *awful* bad. He is *my father!*"

## CHAPTER X

### KATE AND THE GYPSIES

THE fields of ripening wheat and rye looked like lakes of flowing honey, waving and billowing in the wind. They were edged with red poppies and blue cornflowers—beautiful to Kate, but "nasty weeds" to the farmers. Haying was in full swing. The grass on the fields had been cut and piled into tall stacks after it was dry. Some of these stacks would stay on the fields until needed, but the vast haylofts above the barns and stables had to be filled now. Big carts, pulled by lumbering ox-teams, drove in and out of the yard, bringing

136

innumerable loads of hay. Father and Jancsi helped the hired men to store it. They would stand on the high-piled carts and throw big forkfuls of sweet, dry hay into the loft.

Sometimes Kate and Jancsi went out to help load the carts, then rode home nestling on top of the swaying load.

Mother was in the kitchen all day, cooking huge potfuls of stew for the men, baking bread, preserving vegetables. She made jams of the raspberries and blueberries Kate and Jancsi picked for her. Fresh ripe corn was husked and tied into strings, then hung on the porch to dry. These long strings of golden corn looked like necklaces made for giants to wear. The flower garden was in full bloom, repaying Kate's care and hard work a thousandfold.

Harvest time came, bringing long, burning, hot days and silvery, moonlit nights. The harvesters, with their many-colored kerchiefs, shawls, skirts, swaying to the rhythm of the scythe, looked like giant poppies and cornflowers on the yellow fields. Men cut the grain, girls followed them, tying it into neat bundles. They sang happily all day long. It was a good harvest for a "good master," as they called Father.

He was always among them, helping where an extra hand was needed, singing and joking with them. Often he took Kate and Jancsi with him. They carried water to the harvesters, helped to tie and stack the bundles.

Kate noticed that there were many small patches of wheat left uncut. They stood on the smooth fields like little yellow bushes.

"Why don't they cut it smooth and nice?" she asked.

"Come on, I'll show you," said Jancsi. He led her to one of the "bushes." Parting the stalks gently, he whispered: "Look, Kate." There was a nest on the ground with tiny gray birds in it.

"Oh! What are they?"

"Partridges. Father told the men to be careful of the nests. He doesn't want to hurt the baby birds."

The little creatures looked at Kate with their shiny black eyes, unafraid, as if they, too, knew that they were safe on the land of the good master.

Carts and wagons creaked up and down the road, carrying the wheat back to the house to be threshed. The wooden floor of the threshing-house was freshly scrubbed. Stacks of wheat were spread on it. Five or six men were always busy beating— beating the wheat with long wooden flails. After hours of "spanking," as Kate called it, they shook out the straw with pitchforks and tied it into big bundles.

"Bedding for the animals," explained Jancsi.

The clean golden grain left on the threshing floor was shoveled into bags and put away.

"Later on we'll take it to the mill. That's fun, going to the mill," said Jancsi. "The miller is the oldest man you ever saw, Kate, and *he* can tell stories. All about wars and far-away lands."

"Hey, 'farm hands,' " called Father. "Want to help? You can grind up a few bags of straw."

There was a small hand-mill in the barn. Kate turned the handle while Jancsi fed the straw into it.

"What is this for, Jancsi?" she asked, letting the finely chopped straw run through her fingers.

"Bricks. The gypsies will be coming any day now. They make bricks out of clay and chopped straw. Then they burn them in the fire to make them hard."

"Gypsies? Like the musicians at the fair?"

"No. These are traveling gypsies. Oh, Kate, they are queer! The women just look at your hand and tell you everything that's going to happen to you a long time from now."

"Fortune tellers? Oh, but they only make believe, Jancsi. Nobody can tell what's going to happen."

"Well, I don't know about that," hesitated Jancsi. Then he scowled and whispered. "But they can say charms and put a spell on you! Then you have to do what they tell you!" He was round-eyed and very serious.

Kate just shrugged. "Spells! There aren't any spells, Jancsi."

He resented her superior smile. "You just watch yourself! I *know!*"

"Uncle Márton! Come here, please, Uncle Márton," called Kate. "Tell Jancsi that he's talking nonsense. He's been telling me gypsies can put spells on me and make me do things I don't want to do."

Father hesitated. "I wouldn't be too friendly with them, Kate. Perhaps they can't really put spells on you, but they're queer, strange folks. People believe they can work magic. But I *know* one thing," he laughed. "They certainly can take things *off* you if you don't watch sharply. They steal like magpies."

Kate was silent for a while, grinding away busily.

"Oh, well. Ten million gypsies couldn't make *me* do anything I didn't want to do," she said with a grin.

"The current took you and you didn't want to go," grumbled Jancsi.

"Pooh! Gypsies are just people, not water." That was Kate's final word, and no amount of Jancsi's harrowing tales made any impression on her.

The gigantic task of preparing against the long, hard winter went on. Eggs were stored in the cellar, milk made into cheese. Two pigs were getting fatter and fatter. When the first frost came, they would be butchered. Then Mother could make lard, sausages, smoked hams. Wagonloads of oats for the horses came from far fields, sheaves of flax for Mother to make homespun linen. Bags of sheep wool were stored; the dealer from the city would come in the fall to buy wool. To Kate all this was new and fascinating. In the city everything could be had in the stores at any time. Now she saw that every bite of bread meant hard work—months of planning, worry, anxiety. Having had a small share in all this, every bite of bread was all the sweeter to her.

With the first cool days of early fall, potato digging began. Father dug up row after row of the brown roots, Kate and Jancsi filling bag after bag with them. They were just as brown as the potatoes, covered from head to foot with dirt. Jancsi straightened his aching back, stretched his arms. "Kate! Father!" he cried. "Look! The gypsies are coming!"

Four battered, ragged covered wagons were coming slowly

down the road. They stopped a little distance away from the gate.

"Jancsi, you run and tell Mother to get her broken pots and pans ready. I'll be down in a little while. Kate and I will finish up this row first."

Kate wasn't much help, though. She was watching the gypsies. They just *poured* out of the rickety wagons. There didn't seem to be any end to them. In a jiffy they had a campfire blazing and a huge pot hung over it.

Father finished the row and glanced up. "I bet they'll have a few of my chickens for dinner," he said, smiling. "Let's go down before they 'put a spell' on the fattest pig."

When they reached the camp, a swarm of dirty little urchins surrounded them. "Money, Meester. Give the poor gypsies money!"

Father took out a handful of small copper coins and threw them in the air. "Scramble, now," he laughed. The little gypsies became a writhing, screaming mass of arms and legs, fighting for the coins like wildcats.

A very old gypsy came forward, showing all his brilliant white teeth in a friendly grin. "May all the good saints bless you, Mr. Nagy, and you, little Missy." The other gypsy men and women were crowding around them, eying Kate curiously. She didn't like them and pressed close to Father.

"I'll have some work for you gypsies—pots and pans to mend, bricks to make. Get settled now and you can start right in," said Father.

"Sure, sure, Mister Nagy. But maybe you could find a few

scrawny little chickens for us—we are all so very hungry."

Father sniffed. Something was cooking in the big pot. An old woman said hastily: "We found an old hen by the gate—dead." Father laughed. "Was it dead when you found it?"

"Dead now, Mister Nagy—very dead, now," grinned the old crone, rubbing her hands.

"You keep away from my chickens and get busy. Maybe I'll find a sheep for your supper," said Father, turning away to go.

"Sure, sure, Mister Nagy, we keep away, but the chickens just can't keep away from us."

Father was still laughing as they walked back to the house. "They're dirty, thieving, irresponsible good-for-nothings, and yet nobody can be really angry with them. I know they would steal the shirt off my back, but what can I do? They're no worse than the jack rabbits in the corn or the sparrows in the wheat."

"Aren't they queer, though, Uncle Márton? I felt funny when they looked at me with their black eyes," said Kate. "Do you think they can *really* work magic?"

"They can make a chicken disappear quicker than anybody else! Outside of that—don't worry about magic, Kate, only don't go into their camp when you are alone."

Kate found it hard to keep away from the gypsies. Something interesting was always going on in the camp. They made hundreds of bricks for Father and mended every pot, pan, and pail around the house. The women smoked pipes and played cards all day. After dark, they sat around the fire singing strange, sad songs. At night the soft, sweet tune of violins sang Kate to sleep. If they could not work any other magic, they could coax magical tunes out of their battered violins. They could make them laugh with wild gayety, sob and cry with incredible sadness.

The slight fear their dark faces and piercing eyes had roused in Kate wore off quickly. For hours at a time she watched the children romp and dance. She loved their hilarious games. Clad in their own glistening brown skins and very little else, they were carefree and friendly, like a bunch of puppies.

When all the work the gypsies could do was finished, Father offered to pay them. "You can have money or sheep and chickens. What do you want?"

They came to an agreement. They would take four sheep and a dozen chickens.

"Very well," said Father. "I'll drive out and get the sheep and you can have them tonight. Then—on your way, gypsies, I don't want to see you until next summer."

"Sure, sure, Mister Nagy," they said, grinning. "We go, follow the birds to the south."

Father left in the wagon, taking Jancsi with him. Kate was busy picking ripe seeds from her garden, putting them into neat little bags for next spring. She hesitated for a while, whether to go or stay, but decided to finish her job.

On the way to the sheep Jancsi got worried. "Father . . . I don't think we should have left Kate home. They might . . . steal her or something. . . ."

"Don't worry, Son, they won't take her far! She screams

too loud," laughed Father. "Besides, I didn't like to leave Mother alone in the house. Kate can help her watch those nimble-fingered rascals."

At Toepincher they selected the four sheep and started back immediately. It was late afternoon, the sun was going down fast as they came to the storm-fence. The house loomed up in the distance, a mile to go. Somebody was running across the fields . . . why, it was Mother!

"Something went wrong, Jancsi!" cried Father, whipping the tired horses into a fast run. When they reached Mother, she just fell against the wagon, panting, out of breath. She could hardly speak.

"Kate . . ." she gasped. "The gypsies . . . Kate gone . . . the pig . . . chickens . . . *oh, Kate!*"

"Get on the wagon, Mother, and pull yourself together. You can tell us all about it on the way."

"Oh hurry, hurry!" wailed Mother. Little by little she told the story. She was doing her washing by the brook. Kate was in the house, fussing with her seeds. "When I came back . . . she was gone!" cried Mother, wringing her hands. "My honey-lamb . . . they stole her! And the fattest pig is gone . . . and nearly all the chickens!"

Father was very angry. "This is what I get for treating them decently. We'll go after them on the saddlehorses, Jancsi; this time they won't get away so easy. I don't mind a few chickens. We could even do without the pig. But when it comes to taking Kate with them—that isn't funny!"

He drove furiously, not sparing the horses. When they turned in at the gate, the animals were shivering, breathing white foam out of their nostrils, tired out.

"Mother, you take care of them. Come on, Son, let's saddle and get going!" cried Father, running to the stable. Jancsi was right behind him. "Get the lanterns! Mother, you give us some bread and meat. Bring my gun. Hurry! Put the food in the saddlebags. Don't forget some sausages for Kate!"

"Which way will you go?" asked Mother, stuffing generous sandwiches into the saddlebags.

"We'll find their trail, I think they'll make for the mountains. Ready, Son? Let's go then!"

They found the wheel-tracks going north, toward the river. "Just what I thought. They'll run for the mountains every time they get into mischief. We'll have to catch them before they can hide in the woods, or we'll never see them again." Father was worried, he rode faster and faster, peering ahead into the deepening darkness.

"I can't see the tracks, we are going so fast," cried Jancsi.

"Never mind the tracks, Son, they have to follow this road to the ferry. Dig your heels in, we haven't any time to lose."

Jancsi never rode so fast before. The night was black and cloudy. At first he couldn't see anything, but slowly his eyes got used to the darkness. The road was a dim white ribbon; he could see the dark fields and still darker clumps of bushes and trees. Finally they came to the river. The ferry landing was dark and deserted. They dismounted and lighted the lanterns. There were wheel-tracks running in every direction, it was impossible to tell which were left by the gypsy wagons.

"We'll have to separate and scout around a bit. I'll go west, you take the east trail. Shout if you find something—and shout loud!" said Father.

He started to tie the horses to a post, when Jancsi tugged at his sleeve. "Wait, Father! Listen!"

In the silent night they could hear hurried footsteps, running, stumbling, crashing through the underbrush. Father held up the lantern. "Who is there?" he shouted.

There was utter silence for a moment, then: *"Who is there?"* asked a very faint little voice.

"Kate! It's Kate!" cried Jancsi, plunging into the darkness, running toward the voice.

Father was running too. "Is it you, Kate?"

"Oh, Uncle Márton, I'm coming, I'm coming!"

Jancsi reached her first. "It's really Kate, Father!" he shouted, waving the lantern, jumping up and down excitedly.

A very dirty, pale, frightened-looking Kate stumbled into Father's arms, babbling, laughing, crying. He carried her back to the horses. "The pig—they killed the nice pig!" wailed Kate.

"Never mind the pig. Here, sit on my lap. We'll take you home now. Here, here, child, don't cry. Everything is all right." Father held Kate in his lap, stroking her hair.

Jancsi, burning with curiosity, nudged her. "Did they put a spell on you?" he whispered.

"Spell, nothing! I went with them because I wanted to,"

came the surprising answer. They looked at her incredulously.

"You—you wanted *to leave us*—and go with the *gypsies?*" stammered Jancsi.

"*Oh, no!* But I told them I wanted to . . . or they would have tied me up and thrown me into the hayloft. That's what they said!" She snuggled closer to Father. "Oh, they were nasty." Tears rolled down her face again; she shivered.

"Easy, Kate, easy. Don't talk about it now," said Father softly.

"I want to talk, Uncle Márton, I have to tell you—it was awful. I don't know where to begin—my head is going around so. . . ." She yawned and closed her eyes.

"Get on your horse, Jancsi, Kate can ride with me." Father lifted her into his saddle and swung up behind her. She mumbled something. "What did you say?" asked Father.

"I am hungry."

Jancsi laughed. "So am I! Where is the food Mother gave us?"

They rode slowly, eating bread and cold meat. Kate brightened up for a moment when she saw the sausages, but went to sleep after a few mouthfuls. So Jancsi didn't find out until next day how Kate went away with the gypsies.

Soon after Father and Jancsi had left to get the sheep, Mother had called to Kate: "I'm going down to the brook to do my washing. You watch the gypsies, Kate. Call me if they try to steal anything." When Kate had all her seeds put in bags, she went inside to put them away. She looked out the window—there were gypsies all over the place! She saw one of them lead the pig—there were at least six in the poultry

yard catching chickens! She ran out, prepared to call Mother
But she couldn't even open her mouth—somebody clapped
hand over it. It was a husky young gypsy, and he held her so
tight she couldn't move. "Quiet, Missy," he muttered. "We
won't hurt you if you're quiet."

He took her to the wagon and pushed her in, saying something to the women inside. It sounded strange to Kate—he
was talking in gypsy language. She was beginning to get
frightened—all the women crowded around and stared at
her. The children were romping and screaming outside
Mother wouldn't hear her anyway. She was very quiet, waiting for a chance. Through the torn canvas sides of the wagon
she could see the gypsies taking everything they could move
She jumped up, but an old woman pulled her back. She was
grinning at her. "Nice Missy, don't make noise or it will be
bad for Missy."

Soon they were ready to go. "We tie you up now, throw
you in hayloft—can't make noise—we stuff rags in your
mouth," said one of the men. They were all nodding their
heads, laughing.

Kate was thinking hard all this time. Perhaps, if she would
go with the gypsies, she could call for help. She just couldn't
bear to see them get away with the nice fat pig . . . dozens of
chickens, bags of corn and wheat.

"Wait!" she said. "You don't have to tie me up. I won't
scream. But you've got to take me with you!"

They looked at each other. The old gypsy shook his head
"Much trouble if we take you. People are very angry if gypsies
take white children."

"Oh, but I *want* to go. You wouldn't be *taking* me, I want to go with you. I like you. My uncle is making me work for him. I want to run away. Won't you let me come?"

It worked. The women laughed. "Missy don't like work—like music and dancing?"

"That's it, I like music, the way you play the violin," said Kate.

One of the men cried: "He, your uncle, makes much work for gypsies, too. We know! We'll take you, Missy, far, far away. Never work, gypsy girls don't work, just dance and play. Missy make nice gypsy girl, her face all brown now."

They all climbed into the wagons. There were children and chickens and rags. It was so crowded Kate could hardly breathe. She pressed close to the ragged canvas—for air and to see which way they were going. It was the north road—there would be people at the ferry and she could call for help there. They traveled fast all afternoon. It was sundown when they came to the river. She could see the ferry on the other side, but there wasn't a soul around. The wagons turned west, traveling along the river. The mountains loomed up in the distance, the sun disappearing behind them. The road wound around, running into a forest. It was getting dark and Kate was terribly frightened now. What if they didn't stop? Or didn't meet anyone?

They didn't stop until it got very dark. Finally they made camp in a clearing.

Kate heard a long scream and jumped up. "What was that?"

"Nice fat pig for supper," said an old woman, grinning. "Missy hungry?"

"No, I am not hungry now," stuttered Kate. She couldn't eat anything they cooked, they were so dirty. "But I am very sleepy. Could I just stay here and sleep while you are eating supper?"

"Sleep, sleep, Missy. Tomorrow we will be in the mountains, bad uncle never find Missy any more."

"That's just what I'm afraid of," thought Kate and quickly closed her eyes to hide her tears. Maybe if they left her alone in the wagon, she could sneak out and run back to the ferry —call for help—she just had to get away somehow!

"Asleep, Missy?" whispered the old woman.

Kate didn't answer, just peeked once in a while to see if she was alone. The old woman was grinning to herself. In the flickering firelight she looked so much like a witch, Kate shivered. The gypsy woman set a little iron pot on the floor and made a tiny fire in it. She threw something on the fire—a heavy, sickening odor rose from it, making Kate dizzy. A horrible thought came to her as she saw the old hag bending over, making signs and mumbling mysterious words. "If she puts a spell on me! Maybe Jancsi was right and they can really put spells on people!" She was honestly sleepy now. Her head whirled around and around. The old woman snickered: "Sleep, Missy," and left her, closing the canvas curtain at the end of the wagon.

Kate was alone. She moved close to the torn side, gasping for fresh air. Slowly the whirling, sleepy feeling disappeared. She peered out. All the gypsies were sitting around the fire, shouting and singing. Cautiously Kate moved to the curtain. There wasn't anyone around. She stepped down and dropped on her hands and knees, crawling slowly, slowly, always watching the gypsies.

The four wagons stood in a half-circle, and she moved behind them. Then she stood up. It was terribly dark here, and for a while she could see nothing. Slowly her eyes got used to the darkness and she moved on. "If I can only find the road home," she thought desperately, straining her eyes, trying to penetrate the dark forest. She looked around quickly. They were still making merry. Nobody had seen her! She ran, stumbling over roots, bumping into trees.

Then the river glittered between the tree trunks, and soon she was on the open road. She ran, choking, panting, terror-stricken; she ran blindly, desperately. Then—she saw the lanterns—heard Father's voice—felt his strong arms around her—and the nightmarish, awful adventure was over

## CHAPTER XI

## TALL TALES

JANCSI and Kate picked many basketfuls of round red apples. Every last apple was precious; they didn't overlook any. The old tree was free of its burden once more. Then they helped Father cut the dry cornstalks and tie them into neat bundles. Those bundles, standing in even rows, looked like a whole city of small tents. "Houses for the rabbits," Kate called them.

Swallows and storks were preparing to leave. The young birds were strong now and could fly without falling.

"Time to think of wood for the winter," said Father. The patient oxen were put to work again, hauling wood from the forest.

Jancsi and Kate were very proud of each other. Everybody in the village had heard about their adventures. Even the priest praised them. One Sunday, after services were over, he had come out to the church square and stopped to speak to Father. Then he turned to Jancsi and Kate. "You are very brave children; we are all very proud of you. I heard about the round up, and how brave Jancsi was when he saved you in the river, Kate."

"Thank you," smiled Jancsi. "But I was not brave. I was just about scared to death."

"That's just why I call you brave. The best of us are 'scared to death' when we are in danger. But only the courageous stay and fight," said the priest gravely.

"Aren't people nice to us?" sighed Kate happily on the way home. "I wish my father were here, too. It's ever so much nicer than in the city."

"Would you like to stay for good?" asked Jancsi.

"Of course—if I could only see Daddy once in a while."

"Well, Kate," said Father, "I have a surprise for you. I didn't want to tell you now because he won't be here before Christmas, but your father is coming for a long visit. The judge gave me a letter from him last Sunday."

"My daddy!" cried Kate. "Oh, Uncle Márton, I'm so glad. Jancsi, you'll like him ever so much. He's just like Uncle Márton, only not so big and strong."

"Can he ride, too?" asked Jancsi.

"Of course he can ride," laughed Father. "When he was a boy, he almost slept in the saddle. Too bad he ever went to the city."

"Maybe we can make him stay," exclaimed Kate with shining eyes.

"We'll try, Kate, I promise you, we'll try our best," said Father seriously.

Kate was counting on her fingers.

"Oh, it's an awful long time until Christmas. Almost two months!"

"Time will pass quickly. We have a lot to do. The herders are due with the sheep any day now. When they are settled, you can start your school," said Father.

"And you can help me with the flax, Kate," said Mother. "We'll spin and weave on the long winter evenings."

"A pig will have to be killed," said Father.

"And we'll make sausages! Won't we, Auntie?"

Everyone laughed—sausages were Kate's weakness.

The following week the sheep herds came in. The long, low sheepfolds were cleaned. Pista came with his flock, his dog, and his donkey early one morning, and during the day all the other herders arrived. The folds were full of crying lambs, sheep, and rams. There wasn't much work with them and the herders were always ready to help Father. They chopped wood and stacked it high under the shed, helped with the fall plowing, and mended roofs and fences. In the long cool evenings everybody gathered in the big kitchen, around the white stove. Pista carved a beautiful little box for Kate with flowers and lambs on it.

"Now, little lady, if you show me how to write *your* name, I'll carve it on the box. You see, I left a smooth place on it."

All the herders crowded around Kate while she printed her name on a piece of paper.

"Must be wonderful to know what all those little marks mean," sighed Pali, the youngest herder. "To me they look like hen-tracks in the dust! Is it very hard to learn about letters?"

"No, of course it isn't hard. I promised Pista and Jancsi to teach them. We can start right now," cried Kate.

"Who else wants to go to Kate's school?" asked Father.

"We all do," cried the herders.

"Come on, Jancsi, help me find paper and pencils."

She gave everybody a big sheet of paper and a pencil.

"I'll write the letters first and you copy them. We'll begin with the A-B-C like in a real school."

They sat around the big table. Kate began to write.

"Don't give them too much to remember, Kate," said Father. "Three or four letters a day are enough."

"That's right, Uncle Márton! You see"—she turned to her rapt pupils—"this is A—apple begins with an A. The next letter is B, like button, and this is C, like—like ——"

"Corn," cried Jancsi.

"Corn. And this is D, donkey," finished Kate.

"That's easy! I can remember the letters if I know what they mean," said Pista.

They wrote their lesson, murmuring to themselves: "Apple, button, corn, donkey. Apple, button, corn, donkey."

"Now we can make words," said Kate after they had written the four letters several times.

"B, A, and D together like this mean 'bad.' " She wrote down the word. "You read it, Pista."

Pista wrinkled his forehead. "Button, apple, donkey!" he said proudly.

"Oh, no, Pista," laughed Kate. "When the letters are made into words, you don't say 'button, apple, donkey'—just 'bad.' "

"Oh, I know now," he exclaimed. "Like those funny lines you scratched on the floor—they were letters put together like this?"

"That's it, Pista—now read it again."

"Bad!" cried Pista, slamming the table. "I can read! I means bad!"

"Jancsi, you read it backwards; it means another word that way," said Father.

Jancsi looked and looked. Suddenly he jumped up. "Dab!" he screamed. "I can read, too!"

The first lesson was a great success. They would have stayed up all night, but it was getting late. "School dismissed," said Father, smiling, "time to go to bed."

"Tomorrow I'll show you some more letters," promised Kate when the herders said good night.

"Not tomorrow, Kate; if it's windy tomorrow, we'll go to the mill. I'll wake you before sunrise," said Father.

During the night the frost painted everything white. It was dark and cold when they started. Mother tucked heavy sheepskins around them. Two wagons were loaded with bags of wheat. Father drove one and Jancsi the other. Kate sat next to Jancsi, huddled under her sheepskins. She was sleepy and cold, but she wouldn't have stayed home for anything.

For a long time all she could see were the swaying lanterns on Father's wagon. Slowly the black night turned gray, the wind grew stronger, finding every little opening in her covers and clothes, chilling her to the bone. Jancsi's teeth were chattering, his fingers grew red. But when the first rays of the rising sun touched the frosty white plains, all discomforts were forgotten. They were traveling in fairyland. Every branch, every blade of grass, sparkled in the sunshine. The long branches of weeping willows growing on the edge of the brook formed a shimmering archway overhead. Frightened rabbits hopped across the road, peeping at them from under sprays of glistening grass.

They stopped for a minute to put out the lanterns, then drove on, following the winding brook.

"I'm beginning to thaw out," said Kate.

"M-m-m"—Jancsi looked at her—"your nose is still redder than a cherry."

"I wish you could see your own," giggled Kate; "it's a bright blue."

The road turned sharply, the wheels making a hollow rumbling noise as they rolled across a moss-covered wooden bridge.

"There's the mill!" cried Jancsi. Kate sat up, throwing off her coverings. Etched sharply against the blue sky stood a tall, white building shaped like a sugar-cone.

"What's the big pinwheel on it?" asked Kate.

"Pinwheel!" cried Jancsi scornfully. "Those are the vanes. The wind turns them, and they are hitched to the grinding stones inside the mill."

The mill didn't have any windows, just one big door. As the wagons drew up, the door opened and an incredibly old, gnomelike man stepped out. His long hair was white, his eyebrows were white, his clothes were covered with flour. He walked slowly, leaning on a gnarled stick.

"You just unload the wagons, Mister Nagy," he said to Father; "I'll call my helper. I have to have a helper now—I must be getting oldish."

He walked around the mill, to the tiny cottage nestling behind it.

"This is Daniel, Mister Nagy," he said as he appeared again, followed by a husky young giant. Daniel shouldered two bags at a time, running up the steep stairway with them without even breathing hard. The old miller looked on.

"He'll be a good helper when he gets used to the work. When I was his age, I used to carry four-five bags of wheat."

Father winked at the smiling helper. "Last year it was only three bags. If he lives very much longer, he'll tell us he carried a whole wagonload!"

"Old men tell tall stories, Mister Nagy," said Daniel. "Just the other day he told me he once saved the king's daughter from a fire-spitting dragon. He has lived so long and seen so many things, he is getting kind of mixed up. Doesn't know the difference between a fairy tale and the truth."

"Don't stand there jabbering, Daniel," scolded the old miller. "Throw the vanes against the wind and let's start grinding."

They climbed the rickety stairs leading to the top landing. Daniel pressed a hand lever. The big vanes outside opened like a fan and, as the wind caught in them, began to spin. There was a crackling, rumbling noise.

"The stones are moving—feed the wheat now!" cried the old miller, starting down the stairs.

"Keep away from that big funnel, Kate. That's the hopper," said Jancsi. "Watch now, see—they feed the wheat into it. The grains are crushed between the grinding stones."

"Where does the flour come out?"

"Come on downstairs, we can watch it pour in to the bags."

They ran down just as the white flour began to flow out of a narrow chute. Old Miller held a bag under it. The air was thick with the flour dust. Soon they were white from head to toe, like Old Miller himself.

Father came down. "Let me take your place, Old Miller. Daniel said I'm in the way up there." He turned to Kate. "You have seen everything now, Kate, and both of you are quite sufficiently covered with flour. Ask Old Miller to take you outside; maybe he feels like telling you one of his famous stories."

"Now, now, let me see! Will you call me, Mister Nagy, if

you get tired? You young men nowadays aren't as strong as you should be. Why, when I was your age, I could spin the vanes around with one hand—didn't need any wind."

"Oooh! That *was* a tall one!" whispered Jancsi.

"You mean he couldn't really?" asked Kate.

"Of course not. You saw the vanes; they're as big as the mill, and the stones they pull weigh a ton. Nobody could budge those vanes without wind!"

Father reassured Old Miller very solemnly that he would be able to hold the bags.

"So you youngsters like stories, eh?" mumbled the old man as they walked out.

"M-m-m. About fairies and gnomes and dragons," said Jancsi.

"And wars and far-away lands," cried Kate.

Old Miller chuckled. "Well, now, I'll tell you a story that has everything in it."

He led them to his cottage. "Let's sit on the stoop here and I'll tell you about the Land Where People Never Die."

This is the story of Prince Mátyás and his favorite servant, Matyi. Matyi was one of my great-great-grandfathers—I've forgotten which one. There were always too many great-grandfathers in my family, and I'm rather mixed up which is which. Anyway, when the story begins, this Prince Mátyás was just twenty years old. And a big good-for-nothing he was! He was so lazy he wouldn't even button up his coat. Matyi had to do it for him. All he wanted was to have good times, lots to eat and drink, plenty of jesters to make him laugh. He was as cross as a bear, too, and didn't have a friend in the world except Matyi. Matyi just loved him, only he knew why—nobody else did. Prince Mátyás picked fights with all his neighbors, but he didn't fight himself. He sent his soldiers to do the dirty work. Well, to make a long story short, one night he had a dream. Maybe he had eaten too much for supper, but anyway he dreamed about a land where everybody lives forever and ever. He couldn't forget this dream, but kept thinking about it. It made him grouchier than he was before, and even Matyi lost patience with him.

One day he said to the Prince: "With all due respect to Your Highness, and no offense meant, you are getting to be just about intolerable. If you can't forget your dream, let's get on our horses and find that wonderful land. I know it can't be better than our own country, but if it will make you happy, I am ready to go to the end of the world with you."

"Well, Matyi, I never thought of that! Get the horses— we'll start today—right now!"

"Just like that, Prince Mátyás? Just you and I?"

"No back-talk, Matyi! Do what you are told."

"Hm. Anybody would think it was your own idea," grumbled Matyi. But he saddled the horses. Without saying a word to anyone, they rode off.

They rode over fields and pastures, crossed creeks and rivers, passed villages and towns, climbed hills and mountains. Night came and still they rode on. The road became steep and rocky, and the tired horses stumbled over rolling stones. The moon came up, illuminating a strange land. Huge walls of blue-green rocks framed the narrow path. The path ascended steeper and steeper until it seemed to disappear into the dark blue sky.

Matyi couldn't keep still any longer. He sighed.

"I've seen mountains before, but nothing as musty and old-looking as these. Not a wisp of grass on these rocks. Smells oldish, too. This kind of place is for gnomes or goats. The good old plains for me where you can see for miles and miles without bumping your nose into something."

His horse shied. "Hey, Prince Mátyás, look who's here!" Matyi yelled.

An old man stepped out from behind a big rock. He was dressed in a torn old bearskin and had a stone ax in his hand.

"My dear old fellow, what do you call this land, and who in the world lives in a place like this?" asked haughty Prince Mátyás.

"This, young stranger," said the old man, "is called the Land of Work. A great many people live here and they have all lived here a great many years. If you tell me who you are and where you come from, I may tell you more about this land."

Prince Mátyás told him. He also told him what he was looking for. The old man shook his head. "To my knowledge, there is no such land where people live forever. But let me show you our city. You might want to stay with us for a while."

He led the way, skipping from rock to rock like a goat.

The path became steeper, the moon seemed so close that Matyi reached up, trying to touch it. Then the path turned sharply—and there was the city! And what a strange place it was. Grayish green, old, old houses formed a square. The cobblestones on the streets were worn so smooth the horses' hoofs slipped on them. And what strange people! Old and young, ugly and beautiful, they all looked dusty and worn with age. And they were working—all of them. Prince Mátyás and Matyi could see them behind the windows of their ancient houses working, working. Painting pictures, chiseling statues, writing books, bent over looms. Some of them were making lace, others were blowing glass. On the streets they were building houses and constructing bridges. No two of them were dressed alike. They wore costumes of all ages and all nations.

"You see, Prince Mátyás," said the old man, "this is the City of Work. Everybody comes here, that is, everybody who ever made anything which did not perish with them when they died. Some of them, like myself, live here for thousands of years. As long as anything of our work remains in your world, we do not die. I am the man who carved figures on the stone walls of my cave way back in what you now call the Stone Age. I slept for a long time, but a while ago one of your people found my work and now I live again. The builders of the pyramids, the sculptors of Greece, the painters of Italy—they all come here after you say they are dead. But we die only when our work dies. So you see, we really live for very long. Stay here with us, Prince Mátyás, at least for a little while."

Prince Mátyás dismounted. "Thank you for your invitation. We would like to stay and rest for a while. But tomorrow we must go on—and on—until I find the Land Where People Never Die."

The old man shrugged. "Follow me." He led the way to a small house outside the city. It was dusty and old, but somehow it was very familiar.

"Hey! Bless my soul, Prince Mátyás, look at this house," cried Matyi. "If this isn't a peasant cottage from our country, my name isn't Matyi!"

And so it was. Low, whitewashed walls, thatch roof, blue shutters. A Hungarian peasant came out to welcome them. "I built a house like this five hundred years ago, but it is still lived in by my great-grandchildren. It is not very fancy or comfortable, but I welcome you to a good Hungarian gulyás. I always eat gulyás, that's the only thing I can cook."

Matyi looked around. "Can't your wife cook?"

The peasant sighed. "That's just the trouble! My wife never did anything else in her life but cook. And a good cook she was. We ate every morsel of her food. There was nothing left. So she couldn't come here with me."

They had supper, sitting around a worm-eaten oak table. Matyi ate so much, he tossed all night, dreaming about hundreds of little old men clad in bearskins.

Next morning they rode on. Matyi was deep in thought. At length he burst out: "We couldn't have stayed there anyway! Do not take it as an offense, Prince Mátyás, but you haven't done a lick of work all your life."

The Prince smiled. "You know, Matyi, I've been thinking the same thing just now. It will be different from now on. After we find my dream land, we shall return to our country. Then I will work—my people will never forget me!"

Toward noon they came to another city. It was surrounded by a stone wall. Two soldiers guarded the big golden door in the wall. They led Prince Mátyás and Matyi to the King's castle. The King came to welcome them. The Prince told him what he was looking for.

"You came to the right place, Prince Mátyás," said the King. "This is the Land of Friendship. I couldn't say that we live forever and ever, but as long as there is true friendship in your world, we shall not die. Stay here with us. But you must promise me that you will never argue or fight, or even contradict anyone here. We are all good friends, and you must stay friendly with all my people."

"Let's talk this thing over, Prince Mátyás," whispered Matyi.

They said good-by to the King and rode on.

"It sounds good to me, Matyi, we might stay here for a while," said the Prince.

"Hm. Just how many friends have you got, Prince Mátyás? And how long do you think you could stay in a namby-pamby land where you can't fight and you can't argue?"

The Prince laughed. "Right again, Matyi. But why haven't I ever had any friends?"

"Just because you jump down everybody's throat, because

you never help anybody, because you always want to have your own way. That's all!"

"I'll change, Matyi, I'll make friends and keep them when we return home. But first I must find my dream land."

They traveled all day without meeting anyone.

When darkness came, they were just on the edge of a forest. The immense gnarled trees grew close together. Thorny bushes and twisting vines closed every path.

"I wouldn't go in there, even if we could. It's the creepiest place I ever saw," said Matyi. "Let's look for a place to sleep."

"Come to my house, strangers," said somebody.

"Bless my soul! Who are you and *where* are you?" cried Matyi.

"I'm right here, follow me," said the voice.

"Now we know just about as much as we did before. Do you feel like following him, whoever he may be, Prince Mátyás?"

"Ha! so you are Prince Mátyás," said the voice. "I have heard about you and I know what you are looking for. Don't look any more, stay here with me. You will live forever!"

"Who are you?" asked Prince Mátyás.

"I am the Spirit of Hatred. My twin brother is the Spirit of War. We shall live forever and ever! Your people keep us alive with their cruel wars. As long as you fight each other in your world, we shall live and grow stronger and stronger. Follow me. I shall lead you to my house."

"Don't you move, Prince Mátyás," grumbled Matyi. "This cheerful person sounds ugly. Let's look at him first."

"Look at me then—and look at my stronghold," boomed the voice. As he spoke, a sinister red glow illuminated the forest. The horses snorted and shied, and a cry of horror escaped from the Prince's lips. A monstrous-looking creature stood before them. His matted, wild hair almost hid his green eyes. His lips were drawn back, exposing fanglike teeth. Before the light faded, the Prince saw the smoldering charred ruins of a house behind the trees.

"Come on, Matyi, let's get away from here!" he cried. They wheeled the horses around and rode away as fast as the animals could go. When the forest was far behind them, they stopped.

"Matyi, if we ever get home, I'll never, never send my people to war again. Hatred! War! So that's what they look like!"

"I could have told you what they look like without traipsing all over creation. So could your people who fought for you."

"Never again, Matyi, never again will I send them to war. I swear I won't!"

"Hm! Our little trip seems to have been worth while after all, even if we don't find your dream land," said Matyi.

"We shall—we must find it. Maybe tomorrow."

"The first thing *I* am going to find tomorrow will be something to eat," grumbled Matyi before they fell asleep.

He was the first to wake up next morning. "Hey, Prince Mátyás, look! Open your eyes—we are in heaven! Or at least in fairyland. Come on now, get up and wipe your face. It is dirty and people are coming."

Prince Mátyás jumped up. A group of beautiful maidens were coming toward them; with the maidens came a richly dressed old man. He wore a long white cape and had a golden crown on his head. Beautiful flowers grew in their path, gayly colored birds flitted around their heads. They stopped in front of Prince Mátyás and Matyi.

"Welcome, young strangers," said the old King. "Won't you tell me who you are and how you found our garden?"

Prince Mátyás told his story once more. The old King smiled. "So you are Prince Mátyás! I have heard about you. I even know that you were in the Land of Work, that you saw the Land of Friendship, and that you met the Spirit of Hatred. My little fairies travel fast and far. They told me about you."

"Are you King of Fairyland?" asked the Prince.

"I am the King of the Garden of Remembrance. My fairies are Memories. Memory of Peace, Memory of Love, Charity, Good Will. Memories of all the beautiful things in your life. We live long—oh, some of us live very, very long. But forever—Prince Mátyás—even Memories don't live forever!"

"Where then, where shall I find the land of my dreams?" cried Prince Mátyás.

"You are going farther and farther away from it," said the old King. "You must be blind, Prince Mátyás. If the things you saw on your journey failed to open your eyes, if they failed to teach you where you have to go and what you have to do to live forever, I am not going to fail. I shall take you to the land of your dreams."

He clapped his hands. A wonderful winged horse appeared. "Come with me," commanded the King.

They mounted the horse. Poor Matyi clung to Prince Mátyás for dear life. The horse spread its giant wings and rose up, high up above the clouds. They flew higher and higher, quicker than the wind, quicker than the rays of the sun. The clouds parted. The winged horse circled around, then alighted in a green field.

"Here we are, Prince Mátyás, in the land of your dreams."

Matyi looked around with shining eyes. "It looks good— hm, it smells good. Listen! I hear music. Gypsy music. A csárdás! Hey, Prince Mátyás, it sounds good, too."

The old King smiled.

"Prince Mátyás, this is your own country. This is the land where you will never die. Be a good king to your people, be a good friend to your friends, be a tolerant neighbor to your neighbors. Love your people and work for them as they work for you. Then you will live in their memory, in their tales, songs, in their hearts, forever and ever. This is the only place in the world where you can live forever—your own country!"

He mounted his horse and disappeared among the clouds.

Matyi sighed. "I didn't exactly enjoy that flying business on an empty stomach. But he was a wise old King just the same. Let's find something to eat now, don't stand there gaping after him, Prince Mátyás."

The Prince smiled. "He *was* a wise old King, Matyi, a very wise old King. Let us go home!"

"That's what I say," said Father, who had been listening to the old miller's story for quite a while. "Let us go home. The flour is on the wagons and it will be dark before we reach home."

"Thank you for the story, Old Miller, it is the best story I ever heard," said Jancsi.

"You are welcome, Son. May you grow big and strong like I was. Why, a few years ago I used to pick up the whole mill and move it to a different place when I got tired of one spot."

"And that was the tallest story I ever heard," giggled Kate as she climbed into her sheepskins.

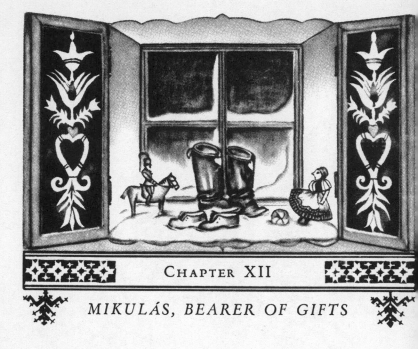

## CHAPTER XII

## MIKULÁS, BEARER OF GIFTS

IT HAD been snowing since last night. The first light flakes fell
just before bedtime, drifting into the yellow shaft of light,
shining through the kitchen window. Kate and Jancsi ran
out trying to catch some of them. It wasn't very cold then,
and the flakes melted as soon as they fell on the ground. By
morning the drifting flakes had changed into a real snow-
storm. Deep drifts had piled up against the walls, and the
barns and stables were just gray shadows behind the veil of
swirling snow. An icy wind howled around the house.

Inside, the house was warm and bright with candlelight. There were huge bowls full of chopped meat and spices on the table. Mother was making sausages. The pig had been killed the day before. Father made a roaring fire in the smokehouse, and hams and shoulders were hung up in the chimney. Kate was busy filling sausages and tying up the ends with cord.

"You know what day it is?" she asked Jancsi with shining eyes. "It's the sixth of December! Mikulás Day! Tonight we'll put our boots on the windowsill and Mikulás will fill them with gifts and candy."

"Did you ever see him?" whispered Jancsi.

Kate shook her head. "I tried often, but I always fell asleep before he came. My father said Mikulás wears a long red coat edged with white fur, a red hat, black shiny boots, and he carries a bag of gifts." She paused for a second, then turned to Jancsi confidentially. "Do you think he is real or only make-believe?"

"I don't know. Let's try to stay awake tonight; maybe we'll catch him," said Jancsi.

Father overheard the conversation. He smiled. "You won't have to catch him. We will go to town and bring him home with us—he wrote me that he would come on the train this time."

"Oh, Father!" Jancsi was delighted. "We'll take the sleigh, won't we?"

"We'll have to. It's snowing harder every minute. Look, it's almost dark now and it can't be more than two o'clock."

Kate's eyes were sparkling. "A sleigh ride—oh, good! I've

never been on a sleigh ride. But Uncle Márton, is Mikulás really coming? I mean, a *real* Mikulás, red coat and bag of gifts and everything?"

Father nodded. "With a big bag of gifts, the best Mikulás anybody could wish for. He's making a special trip for you and Jancsi because you have been such very, very good little farm hands."

Jancsi and Kate were puzzled. They strongly suspected that the red-coated Mikulás, the mysterious bearer of gifts, wasn't real. Nobody had ever met him. He came and went in the night, leaving gifts and happiness behind. Jancsi thought perhaps it was Father who always filled his boots, but now he had said they would actually bring him home from the train! It was all very mysterious.

"When do we start?" he asked.

"Around four o'clock. Pista will do the chores tonight. It's a holiday for you and Kate. We'll put bells on the sleigh and you two put on your Sunday clothes. And, Mother—you will make a good holiday supper for us, won't you?"

"Sausages! Does Mikulás eat regular food? Does he like sausages?" asked Kate.

"He used to love them the last time I saw him!" Father laughed.

"When did you see him, Father?"

"Just twenty years ago," said Father.

Later on Jancsi and Father went out to get the sleigh ready. The snow was so deep they had to shovel a path to the stables. The world was wrapped in snow, even their voices sounding muffled and distant.

Kate was so excited, she had to ask Mother to help her button up her dress. It was a new dress, even prettier than the one Mother had made her for Easter. This one had a blue woolen shirred skirt with white and red flowers embroidered around the hem. A tight little blue jacket edged with lamb's fur went with it. The jacket had red buttons all the way down the front. Kate, with her little fur cap and red boots, looked as pretty as a picture. Jancsi had a new winter suit, too. It was exactly like Father's suit—blue wool, the coat lined with fur, and even the brass buttons on it the same as Father's.

When Father came in to carry out the sheepskins, he smiled at Kate. "I think your—er—I think Mikulás will have a great surprise tonight. Look at our 'delicate' Kate, Mother! Isn't she the picture of health? He'll never know her!"

"He never saw me before, Uncle Márton. I was always in bed when he came."

Mother laughed and shook her head. "Father, Father. You'll spoil the surprise if you don't watch out. Here's your hat now. One—two—three—out with you or you will be late for the train."

She came out to tuck the covers around them. It was bitterly cold. When Kate looked around as the sleigh turned onto the road, all she could see was the bright square of the kitchen window. Everything else—house, barns, stables—were blotted out. Soon the sleigh was traveling in a dark no-man's land. The sleigh bells were cheerful; without them there would have been utter silence. The lanterns were comforting; without them there would have been utter darkness.

"One more day like this and we will be snowed in," said

Father. Nobody answered. Kate and Jancsi were snuggled deep under the sheepskins.

Only the dim lights of many small windows told them that they were driving through the village. The street was silent and deserted. Even the town was a very quiet place tonight. Father left Jancsi and Kate in the sleigh and went into the station to see if Mikulás had arrived.

"Oh, Jancsi. I'm so excited I can hardly sit still," whispered Kate. "Do you think he is really coming?"

"Father said he was coming—so he *is* coming!" said Jancsi stoutly. But he watched the door just as anxiously as Kate. They heard the train come in—stop—then puff and groan again and go. People came out, got into the few waiting sleighs and coaches, and drove away. Then the street was empty again, with only the wind howling around the dark buildings.

"Here they come," cried Kate. Father and Mikulás walked toward the sleigh. They were carrying big bags over their shoulders.

"Mikulás," whispered Jancsi, peering eagerly at the mysterious figure. "He *must* be the real Mikulás—red coat, red cap, black boots, just like his pictures!"

Kate nodded. "And look, he has long white hair and a white beard. He looks very old."

Father lifted the bags into the sleigh. Then he turned to Mikulás. "Now my dear—Mikulás—you had a long, cold trip. We'll just let Jancsi do the driving. You and I will sit in the back and talk about old times."

Mikulás looked at Kate intently, but he did not say anything. He climbed in next to Father, and Jancsi started the

horses. Jancsi was more puzzled than ever. His father was talking to the mysterious Mikulás as if he were talking to a regular everyday man. Kate wiggled on the seat—she kept turning around trying to see the face of Mikulás. But it was very dark. Besides, if she stretched her neck too far out of her sheepskin, the wind stuck a very unpleasant icy finger down her back.

When they reached the village, Father leaned forward. "Stop at the church square, Jancsi. Mikulás has gifts for the village children. He will leave something at every house."

The houses were dark. Village people go to bed early in the winter. Father gave Jancsi and Kate lanterns to carry. He and Mikulás took the big bags and they walked to the nearest house. Then for the first time Mikulás spoke. His voice was strangely muffled. "Hold up the lantern, Kate, let me see my list."

He produced a long sheet of paper. "Hm! Two children

in this house, good children, too. What do you think they would like, Jancsi? Open the big bag, let's see what we have."

The bag revealed an astonishing assortment of gifts. Toy animals, dolls, pocketknives, bags of candy, warm stockings, mittens, boxes of crayons, books, small tools, games—everything to make children happy.

Jancsi was thinking hard. He knew every child in the village. These two were girls—one of them three years old, the other six. "Dolls—I think they would like dolls best—or perhaps some candy."

They found the little shoes on the windowsill. Kate put a small doll near each shoe *and* a little bag of candy. Slowly they walked from house to house.

"Isn't this just wonderful, Jancsi?" whispered Kate. "It makes me feel all warm and good inside."

"Me, too. It's better than the fair."

They came to the very last house. There were two worn little shoes on the windowsill, but the big bags were empty. Mikulás looked at Kate. "I haven't anything more, only the gifts I brought for you and Jancsi. We'll have to go home," he said in his strange muffled voice.

"Oh, oh, no, please!" cried Kate. "I would rather leave my gifts here, wouldn't you, Jancsi?"

"I would! Please, Mikulás, won't you let us give our things to these children? We—we had a wonderful time anyway, just going around with you."

Mikulás didn't say a word. He brought a small package from the sleigh. There were two pairs of warm mittens in the

package, two big picture books, two boxes of candy, and, best of all, two beautiful riding whips. He handed them to Jancsi. Jancsi looked at them longingly for a second. He looked at Kate. But he shook his head. He remembered the two boys in this last house. Their father was the poorest man in the village. Then he smiled at Mikulás. "These are beautiful gifts, but these are very poor children. Thank you for letting us leave them here."

Mikulás made a queer noise in his throat. It was something between a laugh and a sob. When he spoke, his voice was huskier than ever. "Thank you, Jancsi, and thank you, Kate. You have made me very happy tonight."

Kate squeezed Jancsi's hand. On the way back to the sleigh she whispered to him: "I have heard his voice before—only I can't remember where. You know, Jancsi, I just *can't* believe that he is the fairy-story Mikulás. He sounds too real!"

"I think so, too," said Jancsi. "But tonight feels like a fairy story just the same. Father looks like he always does when he has a big surprise for us. Anything might happen!"

Wisps of conversations came from the back of the sleigh: "Gypsies—round up—sausages—Milky." Father was telling Mikulás about Kate and Jancsi. A hearty laugh made Kate turn around quickly, and just as quickly it changed into a hoarse cough. Where had she heard that laugh before?

Mother must have heard the sleigh bells because she was standing in the open door as they reached the gate. Pista was waiting for them. "I'll take care of everything, Mister Nagy. You just stay with the family tonight."

The table was set beautifully; it was a blaze of candlelight and color. There was a roaring fire in the big stove. Mother wore her best Sunday clothes, too. She came forward now, smiling happily. "Welcome home, Mikulás," she cried. And to the astonishment of Kate and Jancsi gave him a good hug and kiss. "Here, sit by the fire and get warm. I'll have supper on the table in a minute."

"Thank you, my dear. It does feel like coming home at last," said Mikulás.

"Daddy!" screamed Kate, running toward him. "You are —you *are* my daddy! Take off your hat, please. And those white whiskers. Now I know where I had heard your voice before. Oh, Daddy!"

The rest was mumbled against the shoulder of Mikulás, who held Kate very close to him, while Mother, half laughing, half crying, tried to peel off his false white hair and beard.

When he finally discarded all his Mikulás disguise, Kate's father looked startlingly like his brother. He had the same strong, kind face, the same honest, merry eyes. He held out his hand to Jancsi. "Come here, Son, let me take a good look at you."

Jancsi advanced cautiously. He liked his uncle very much at first sight, but perhaps he would want to kiss him, or something—men didn't kiss each other! But no—Uncle Sándor shook hands with him gravely and did not attempt to make a baby of Jancsi.

"I am very glad you came, Uncle Sándor. It's much nicer to have you than to have Mikulás." Then he smiled at Father.

"I knew you had a secret, Father, you had your surprise face on—kind of twinkling and shining all over."

Uncle Sándor laughed. "I had the hardest time trying to change my voice, and those whiskers were a punishment. They tickled my nose so."

"We didn't know what to think, did we, Kate? But honestly, Father, is there a *real* Mikulás?" asked Jancsi.

"You know who the real Mikulás is? He is a different person to every child. He is always the one who loves you best in the world. We left beautiful gifts for the village children, but each of them will find some other gift, too, tomorrow morning. Perhaps it will be a very, very simple little gift, but it will be precious to those children because it was given with the greatest love."

"But who is he, really?" persisted Jancsi. "Just somebody in a fairy story?"

"No, Jancsi," said Kate's father. "I'll tell you who the real Mikulás was. His name was really Nicholas. He was a bishop in Russia about fifteen hundred years ago. While he was alive he used to go around doing good, helping people—he always had a gift for children. He did so much good in his life that after he died people called him Saint Nicholas. Then they made him patron saint of Russia and the patron saint of all children. His day, which is the sixth of December, became a holiday in Russia. They celebrated his day by giving each other, and especially the children, whom Saint Nicholas loved so much, beautiful gifts in his name. This habit spread all over the world. In some countries he comes on Christmas Day.

To us he comes today. We believe that on Christmas Eve the Christ Child walks on earth and leaves gifts for every-body."

Kate looked up. "He does, really, doesn't he, Daddy?"

Kate's father smiled. "He does really, Kate, my dear. He comes, and puts love and tenderness in our hearts, so much love for each other that it overflows and turns into gifts we find under the Christmas tree."

"I think it is beautiful—the way you tell it, Daddy. Now I understand it. It isn't just secrets and make-believe like sometimes I thought it was."

Mother put a steaming dish on the table. Kate sniffed. "Sausages, Daddy, fresh sausages! I helped to make them!"

"And I am as hungry as a bear," laughed her father.

They ate supper and talked long afterwards until the candles burned low and it was time to go to bed. Father opened the door and looked out. It was still snowing silently, steadily. "Might as well make up your mind for a long visit, Brother, the snow will keep you home for Christmas if nothing else will."

They all looked at Uncle Sándor. He laughed.

"We cannot fight against Nature, can we, Brother Márton? But it isn't the snow that will keep me home. The reason is right here, snoring on my shoulder. Where is her room?"

He carried the sleeping Kate toward the door Jancsi opened for him.

"Good night, Uncle Sándor," Jancsi whispered. "I hope it will keep on snowing so you can't ever go away again!"

## CHAPTER XIII

## CHRISTMAS

JANCSI had his wish. All night it snowed and for a week afterwards, steadily. Drifts reached the windows, covered gates and fences, made the road impassable. Every morning and night the men had to shovel new paths from the house to the out-buildings. Soon the paths were like deep canyons between walls of snow. By the time it stopped snowing, the walls were so high Jancsi completely disappeared between them.

With Uncle Sándor and the shepherds to help him, there

was very little for Father to do. One morning he brought in his woodworking tools. "We need some new chairs, Mother," he said. Jancsi helped him find well-seasoned, dry maple planks in the woodshed. Uncle Sándor shook his head and smiled. "So you still make your own furniture! I don't see how you have patience for it when you can buy furniture so cheaply now."

Father grunted. "Glued and nailed factory rubbish. I want furniture we can *use,* not rickety stuff like that. Besides, I have nothing else to do now, shall I twiddle my thumbs and look at the snow?" He measured and cut out seats and backs, rungs and legs, for future chairs.

Uncle Sándor looked on for a while. Then he grew restless. Suddenly he exclaimed: "I haven't had an honest tool in my hands since I left for the city. Got a spare saw, Brother?"

Father laughed. "I knew you couldn't resist it, Sándor, there isn't a man who can resist the song of the saw."

Soon Uncle Sándor was working, humming and whistling to himself. Evenings, the shepherds helped, too. One by one the rough pieces were planed and whittled, smoothed and rubbed down. Leisurely, carefully, painstakingly, they worked until each piece fitted the other perfectly. Then they were fastened together with wooden dowels.

Father threw himself on the first complete chair with all his weight. "Built for a lifetime!" he exclaimed with satisfaction.

Mother was teaching Kate to spin. In the fall, a little after harvest time, she had prepared the flax. Kate told her father how it was done. "We soaked it first, Daddy, soaked it in big tubs for two days. Then dried it in the sun. Later on Auntie showed me how to break the hard fibers in the flax. She has a machine—it works like a clothes-wringer, only you don't roll the flax in it, but work it up and down like scissors. Then we tied the flax in sheaves and combed it out with a wire comb to make it all smooth and even. Here it is, Daddy, on the spinning wheel. See, I can make a nice long thread!" She could, too; the thread she made was just as thin and even as Mother's.

Uncle Sándor looked at Mother. "What have you done to the child, my dear? I sent a spoiled, cranky, pale little girl to you. I find a husky, happy, busy little farmer. She will never fit into city life again!"

Kate stopped the spinning wheel and sat in his lap. "Daddy, I don't want to go back to the city. Can't we just stay here for good? Please!"

"But, Kate. Your education—my work . . ." Uncle Sándor turned to Father, who was looking at them gravely. "What future would she have here, without schools, miles away from civilization?"

Father smiled. "You are a schoolteacher, aren't you, Brother? Well, here is Kate, here is Jancsi, here are these young shepherds, eager to learn. The schoolmaster in the village is so old he can't really teach any more. You could take his place. Wouldn't it be beautiful if you could bring learning and civilization to all these people? Your own people?"

Pista was listening to all this with much interest. Now he

spoke. "Don't take the little lady away from us, Mister Nagy. Stay here with her. You are earning money with your work now, I know. Here, you wouldn't be paid in money—you would earn love and peace and happiness!"

Kate slipped off her father's lap. Her face was shining. She was standing in the middle of the room straight as an arrow. "You remember what you told us, Pista, when I first saw you? I remember every word of it. Listen, Daddy, 'The sky gives me sunshine and rain. The ground gives me food and water. The sheep give me clothing and my bed. The beautiful flowers and animals show me what to carve with my knife. Can money and schools give me more?' That's what he said, Daddy. He gave me this necklace."

"And you showed me how to write my name," interrupted Pista.

"That's how Kate's school started," laughed Father.

"Kate's school? What is that?" asked Uncle Sándor.

"Oh, we never told you about it, Brother, did we? Since you have been here the lessons stopped, the boys didn't want to disturb your visit. Kate has taught Jancsi and the shepherds to read and write. Made a good job of it, too!" said Father proudly.

Uncle Sándor was speechless. He looked from one to the other. Then he began to walk up and down, deep in thought. They watched him anxiously. Minutes passed. He stopped and looked at Father.

"I don't know what to do. Give me a week to think it over, Brother Márton."

"A week? You will have half the winter to think it over.

Mountains of snow don't melt in a week," laughed Father.
"But that reminds me, Christmas Eve is a week from tonight.
Where will we get a Christmas tree?"

This was a puzzle. It was impossible even to attempt a drive
to the mountains where the pine trees grew.

"We'll have to do without one, but it won't feel like Christmas," said Mother sadly.

"I could *make* one," proposed Pista.

They thought he was joking; how could anyone *make* a
Christmas tree?

"I'll tell you how. I will carve out the trunk and branches
—then we can dye some straw green, cut it into small pieces,
and glue them on the branches."

"Or we could paint paper green and cut it into long narrow
strips with frilled edges," cried Kate.

"And we can trim it with popcorn. I'll make some small
cookies and we can tie those on, too," said Mother eagerly.

Everybody had a new idea. "I am glad we can't get a real
tree—this will be much more fun," said Jancsi.

Next day Pista had his tree ready. They pasted strips of
green paper on the branches, and some colored straw, too.
Kate and Jancsi made long strings of popcorn. Mother gave
them strawberry juice from her preserves and they dipped
part of the corn into that and had red and white strings.
Mother made cookies and she polished small apples. They
would go on the tree, too.

Father fitted the tree into a high stand he carved. Uncle
Sándor cut little angels and intricate chains out of colored
paper. Everybody helped to make it beautiful. Long candles

were cut into short pieces and fastened on the tree with wires. The day before Christmas, Mother and Kate trimmed it. "It's more beautiful than any tree I ever saw in the city," cried Uncle Sándor when it was finished.

Mother, of course, found time to cook and bake and roast a wonderful supper. Kate set a real holiday table with the best pottery, a snow-white tablecloth, blazing candles, and a big bowl of red apples for the centerpiece. All the shepherds were invited for the evening.

Darkness fell early. It was Christmas Eve. When everything was ready, Jancsi went out to call the shepherds. In a little while they came, led by the oldest of them. He brought a gift. It was a small scene of Bethlehem, all carved of wood. The Christ Child in a tiny manger filled with straw, Mary and Joseph, the angels, the shepherds, the three wise men, the oxen, and the donkeys were all there. He set it under the tree tenderly and turned around. "Blessed be the house of our good master and everybody in it," he said.

Father shook hands with him. "Thank you, and God bless every one of you, my boys. Sit down now—supper is ready."

It was a merry meal. Kate's father kept the shepherds spellbound as he described the electric lights, automobiles, telephones, radio—the life in the city. They listened eagerly, like children to a fairytale. After supper, Father lighted the candles on the tree. He put out all the others on the table. Then he opened the door wide. "Welcome, Christ Child," he said. Through the open door, across the silent fields, came the faint but crystal-clear voice of the village church bells.

Uncle Sándor stepped to the door. "Silent night, holy night," he said softly. Kate's clear little voice rose, singing "Silent Night, Holy Night"; then Mother took up the tune, then all of them were singing it.

When the song was ended, they sat around the blazing stove, leaving the door open. Outside it had stopped snowing, and the sky was glittering with silvery stars. For a little while everybody was silent, there was utter peace and contentment in the room. Now and then the plaintive cry of lambs came from the sheepfolds, or a cow would moo softly in the barn.

"Next week, if you can spare some wood, Mister Nagy, I'd like to make new feeding racks. We have more sheep this year than ever before. They are crowded," said Pista.

Father nodded. "There is plenty of wood in the shed. I'll help you."

"One of you will have to carve a new bobbin for my weaving-frame. Kate and I will start to make linen next week," mused Mother. "And put in more flax next year, Father; my sheets are wearing out."

"I'd like to make a nice tablecloth too—with red hearts and white doves all around the edge!" sighed Kate.

"That pattern takes a very long time, Kate; we have only one frame."

"We could build another one for the little lady," spoke Pista.

"I'd like to build one for her," said Uncle Sándor. "Remember the one you and I made for our mother, Márton?"

Father turned his head slowly and looked at him. "That

THE GOOD MASTER

took a long time to make, Brother. We worked on it for months and months—maybe a year."

Uncle Sándor smiled. "I know. Maybe a year, maybe more. Every little piece carved and polished. That's the kind I'll build for Kate."

"May I help you, Uncle Sándor?" asked Jancsi.

"Of course. Jancsi and I can have it ready for you, Kate— we can have it ready for next Christmas."

Kate, who was curled up in his lap, giggled. "Please say that again, Daddy. Say it very loud, so we can all hear you!"

"I said, we can have it ready for next—" Uncle Sándor stopped and looked at Father, who was laughing too. "Yes— yes, Sándor, go on!"

Kate sighed and snuggled down contentedly. "You don't have to *shout*, Daddy, we knew it all the time."

"Knew what, you little imp?"

"That you'll stay home—with us!"